THE FIRST CIRCLE

DEVIL IN THE WATERS

BOOK ONE

KT MORRISON

ABOUT THE AUTHOR

KT Morrison writes stories about women who fall in love with sexy men who aren't their husband, and loving relationships that go too far—couples who open a mysterious door, then struggle to get it closed as trouble pushes through the threshold.

Visit My Website!
ktmorrison.com

This is a work of fiction. Similarities to real people, places, or events are entirely coincidental.

Models on cover are meant for illustrative purposes only.

All characters are over the age of eighteen.

THE FIRST CIRCLE

A Devil In The Waters Novella

Book 1

31,000 words

First Edition. January 24, 2020.

Copyright © 2020 KT Morrison

Written by KT Morrison

Cover by KT Morrison

1

DREAMSCAPE

The dream began as though he were waking.

The coarse whisking of the tent's zipper roused Josh from a shallow, painful sleep. Dawning blue-gray light assaulted his eyeballs with the intense zap of high-beam flashlights. He winced and hissed, brain exploding with sharp stabbing pain. His neck throbbed, his brain throbbed, his back was sore.

While bewildered, there was still a strange sense of place. The tent's zipper gave it away; the awful sleep; the cold; the damp. . . . He lay on a thin camping sheet, inside a sleeping bag that was zipped down to his knees, early morning chill stinging his hot, sweaty skin.

Now the tent was jostling, the nylon tapping and

dancing as someone came in. He reached instinctively for Kimmy, aware of a large shape looming over top of them that made him think of a grizzly bear.

"Kimmy, Kimmy," he hissed, hand snatching outward, trying to grab at his wife. She wasn't there. His eyes fluttered open, and he looked now to see that large shape crouched at the tent's door and zipping it closed again with a sharp, quick tug.

"What the hell?"

The figure turned, scooting down and squatting, taking Kimmy's spot next to him. He blinked, clutched at his temples to push away the throbbing pain, trying to make sense of this.

The figure wasn't a bear, but a man. Familiar yet unfamiliar, distant yet right here in front of him . . . His brain flexed and twisted, trying to make sense. As the man's features came into focus, things began to fit into place. Devlin Stone. Dalton High. Class of '09. Football. Lacrosse. Six-foot-two. Handsome as shit. Bully. "Stone?"

The figure said, "Waters, it's done. Holy shit."

He worked up onto an elbow, pain shooting up his collar. He rubbed the back of his neck with his hand. "What the fuck is going on?"

"Waters, you were not fucking kidding."

"Kidding about...? What's happening?"

Stone frowned, brow working low, focusing on sleepy Josh, making Josh feel small and transported back to the frightening halls of Dalton High. It was one small piece of a larger puzzle. Now he began to comprehend the hazy periphery of this dreamy story. On waking, he'd thought he was camping with Kimmy. He wasn't. A reunion. . . . A *high school* reunion. The ten-year reunion. Everyone gathering after the party in the gymnasium at Dalton for a weekend bash at Tiffany Hanson's lakeside cottage. *Bring your tents, bring your own booze!* And he'd had a lot of booze, hadn't he? His stomach was at once held in a vice and simultaneously a luscious, squirming thing. Acid burned, things rolled over inside him. He wanted to barf, burped instead, tasted bourbon.

"God," he said, "what time is it?"

Stone said, "It's almost five. Oh, wow, dude," then ran a big hand through his head of thick black shining hair, "that was close. I almost got caught. . . . Although..."

"Caught what?"

"It was cold out here. We went inside but we got caught in the can."

"What does that mean? *Caught in the can?*" Nothing made sense right now.

"The bathroom. Kimmy's friend caught us. What's that one? . . . I don't remember her name."

"Who? Caught what?"

"Dude. What we talked about. . . . It's done."

Josh nodded, afraid to irritate Devlin by still straying behind. Best to agree and wait for the storm clouds to blow over. "Oh, okay."

Devlin scowled, but seemed amused, which was a relief. "You're not getting it, bro." Now he shook his head and chuckled, "Holy shit, Waters, I'm so glad I sat down and talked to you last night."

"What do you mean?"

"Waters, man, wake up," Stone said and laughed. "You want to hear about it or not?"

"Yes, I want to hear about it—hear about what?"

Stone studied him, a puzzled look on his face. He was an arrogant asshole, never a friend of Josh's. Through the early part of high school and public school, Devlin had been a bully. There were a lot of times where he'd made Josh's life miserable. There was even a time when Josh's own mom and dad marched him down to the Stone household to tell Devlin's uber-rich father what his son was up to. Only Papa Stone didn't care. Smug asshole. When Josh and his parents went home that night, his mom broke a glass in the sink she was so mad. "Fucking prick," she'd called Devlin's father, and Mom *never* swore. That was Papa Stone. Young Devlin Stone had always been on the path to full *Fucking Prick* status.

Devlin said, "Are you kidding me?"

"Kidding about what?"

"Dude, right out there," Devlin said, pointing at the closed door of the tent. "That picnic table right up back of your SUV. You and me last night, God, I don't know, one in the morning...?"

"Oh yeah," Josh said, not really remembering, but not wanting to infuriate big Stone. Even at twenty-eight years old now, the guy packed a whack more solid muscle than he had in high school. He had a big frame, large hands, a square jaw.

"Well, it's done."

"Good," Josh said.

Devlin tilted his head like he would look out the tent's door though it was zipped closed. The muscles in his stubbly jaw flexed as he smiled. "She's still inside, but I'm telling you—we might have got busted."

"What do you mean, busted?"

"Got caught."

Josh nodded, but the act of moving his head too fast got him swooning with sudden seasickness. He burped, said, "Who's inside?"

"Kimmy. . . . What the fuck is wrong with you?"

"Oh, yeah, okay," he said. "Kimmy's inside."

Devlin scowled at him. "How much did you drink last night?"

"I don't even remember."

"We would've gone again—fuck, a bunch of times —but she shooed me out of there because there were people up in the kitchen."

"Shooed you out of where?"

"We went in that bathroom, the one on the main floor just past the family room..."

"Who? . . . You and Kimmy?"

Devlin shook his head. "You really don't remember?"

"No. . . . Maybe..."

"Out on the picnic table," Devlin said, scooting a

little closer so he wouldn't have to raise his voice. "You and I had a talk..."

"What did we talk about?"

Stone moved closer so he could whisper and be heard. Josh could see the cold blue steel of Devlin's eyes. He smelled like sweat and something else. . . . Devlin said, "You told me your fantasy of Kimmy having sex with another man."

Josh's eyes narrowed in incredulous challenge. "I did not."

"Don't pull this now," Devlin said, plucking at the sleeping mat he lay on. "I knew you would do this."

"What are you talking about?"

"Last night you told me about your fantasy Kimmy would have sex with another guy, and I joked I *always* had a fantasy of being with Kimmy ever since high school. You told me to do it, you told me you *wanted* me to do it."

Josh's heart began to pound in his chest; his neck swelled with pulsing blood. As it hit his brain and temples, it felt like his head exploded. He winced, lurched forward, held his stomach. Everything in him wanted to come right back out again. He was still drunk, still full of whiskey. . . . That *had* to be it, because there was no *way* this was real. This had to be a hallucination.

"No. . . . I didn't. . . . That's impossible."

"You did. You told me to, and I thought you were kidding at first, but you were so serious. I mean, the idea isn't *that* crazy. . . . Once you crashed, I laid it on your wife and, Josh, she was an eager little bunny rabbit."

Josh frowned and moaned, wanted to fight back and knew what he was hearing was ridiculous. Devlin taunting him was nothing new, but this crossed a line. You could taunt him—the man—but Devlin's reference to his wife was off limits. Try as he might to formulate a response, instead Josh's cheeks hollowed, his lips pursed, and he faced a strong interior desire to hurl. He closed his eyes; still felt the world spinning.

"I've never seen anything like it, Josh. I'm still *rock* hard right now. If there weren't so many people around, I would be in there going round three with her."

His voice was a tight squeeze as his insides clenched. "Round three?"

"Kimmy can really go. Makes me wish I'd fucked her in high school."

"No way," Josh said, leaning back, putting his hand over his heart, feeling its ridiculously high rate.

"I am like a fucking crowbar right now," Devlin said, rubbing the top of his head and raking back his thick shock of black hair. "Shit, maybe we should get out of here, go get breakfast somewhere and I'll take her into the bathroom."

"No, no, no, no," Josh muttered, head nodding forward as his eyes closed, his mind reeling with disbelief at the absurdity of what was happening and what he was hearing. "What are you... Why are you even *saying* this?"

Devlin grunted. "Look at this," he said and when Josh opened his eyes, Stone's steely gaze was locked on his, chin nudging downward indicating for Josh to look. Josh's eyes moved down Stone's masculine chest, the man's muscle stretching out a plain black T-shirt. A thumb hooked in the front of his sweatpants shorts, pulling them outward; Devlin wore no underwear, and from a nest of thick black pubic hair, his huge tree trunk of an erection protruded. It was massive, twice as long as Josh's, and thick as a woman's wrist. It was a darker brown color than Devlin's already tanned skin, and a meager foreskin retracted over a shining purple-gray helmet the size and shape of a ripe plum. "Josh," Devlin said, "your wife is *so* tight."

A small groan creaked in Josh's throat; lightning flashes shimmered in the corners of his vision. The urge to retch came in again like a wave, washing up the back of his throat like sea water on a nighttime beach. He swallowed, blinked, shook his head and narrowed his eyes on that awful part of Devlin Stone revealed to him. The whole thing farcical yet not unfamiliar. It was unreal that a man was in his tent showing him his erection, but simultaneously, this was not his first time seeing Devlin's penis. All through school Devlin Stone took great glee in swanking his endowment around to all the other boys and enjoyed in ribald comparison of his size to any poor shower-goer caught peeking at his extra-large penis or accidentally making eye contact. Or sometimes only because he was a cruel asshole.

Josh closed his eyes and turned his head away. Stone persisted. "Feel it," he said.

Eyes still closed, Josh scoffed, grunted, "What—why?"

"Feel how hard it is, Josh."

"Just get out of here," he moaned, his head nodding, his mind softly riding imaginary waves that lurched his stomach, Devlin just a voice in his head.

"Come on, little Joshy, put your hand on it. I have a reason."

"Mm, I'm not doing that."

"Give me your hand," the gravelly voice said. Stone's large hand closed on Josh's wrist, guiding his hand lower. From a lifetime of acquiescence, Josh allowed himself to be manipulated; and soon his fingers closed mid-shaft around Devlin Stone's massive erection. It was hot and gummy in the middle, the girth surprising his grip. He shut his eyes tighter and complained in his throat.

Devlin said, "Kimmy makes me so hard, Josh. . . . I wish there weren't so many of her friends creeping around the house."

Josh loosened his grip, moved to pull his hand away, but Stone still held him in place by the wrist. Josh said, "Are you kidding me?"

"No, why would I be kidding you?"

Josh opened his eyes in thin slits, saw Stone leering close. He whispered, "Did you have sex with my wife?"

Stone waited a moment, drawing in an easy breath, then exhaling. "You told me to, Josh."

"You really didn't have sex with her, did you?" His voice was high and pleading, thin with disbelief.

Devlin smiled. "Here," he said, "smell your hand," guiding Josh's wrist back up to his face. Josh recoiled, groaned and closed his eyes, but Devlin pushed the hand closer. He submitted, opening his hand and smelling the palm.

"You smell pussy? That's Kimmy's pussy, right?— you gotta recognize it."

Now he didn't want to smell it, recoiling further, collapsing onto his back, his head missing the pillow and knocking into the thin camping sheet over hard ground. It was enough to send him over the edge. Brand new pain oscillated through his body in radiating waves from the crown of his skull. His stomach tightened, and he tasted bile in his throat. But in his nose was the smell of sex. Whether it was his wife's insides was indecipherable; it was just the funky body-smell of sex—and it was *impossible* that Kimmy had sex with Devlin Stone. A strange hot stone of jealous rage and hurt throbbed in his heart now, his tormentor's lies getting in his head and working their magic.

Near his ear, he could hear Devlin's whisper: "I got balls deep in her, Josh. Balls deep. You should have heard her—bet she never made a sound like that before."

"Go. . . . Jus' get out. . . . Fuck outta here." His weak voice slid out on an exhale, and his hand faffed outward to push Devlin away—but careful not to be forceful as any force would be met with double in return. Those were long-established rules.

But his hand met nothing, only air next to him. He made a soft crying sound as his temples boomed with a throbbing ache. One eye squinted open. Devlin was still there, up on his knees now, unzipping the tent's door, the front of his shorts humped out by his massive erection, muscles in his arms bulging as he worked the zip, then peeked out into the dawn. He glanced Josh's way, smiling.

Josh said, "I don't believe you."

Devlin shrugged, unaffected, unconcerned with convincing. He said, "You made a deal with the devil last night."

"I didn't make a deal with you."

"You did, my friend. We have a contract, and it's open-ended."

"We don't have any contract, Devlin. Just tell me you didn't. It's just crazy, okay...?"

"I did what you wanted, Josh. I'm going to do it again."

"I don't want that."

"Kimmy wants it, believe me. Like I said, if there weren't her friends around the house right now, I'd have her knees up over my shoulders, dumping in her guts. She begged me to come inside her."

That crossed a line, and for the first time, Josh was roused to anger. But his body was pinned to the earth, his eyes fading closed even while his heart burned with rage. He said, "That's not fucking funny—that's *not* fucking funny, you asshole." There was no way Kimmy could've asked for that. This was taunting; this was bullying. And Stone didn't know how low he'd gone.

Kimmy's a dirty little slut, Josh. Your wife's a dirty girl."

"Get out of here," he hissed, the force making his ears ring.

"This is your fantasy, Josh. You started it."

"You didn't really do it. Kimmy didn't do it. You're just an asshole."

"Keep telling yourself that, Waters," Devlin said, getting up on his knees now, poking his head to the outside and looking around. He ducked back in. "Kimmy says you're out in Ajax now."

"So?"

"I get through there at least three times a month."

"So?"

"So I'll be seeing you." With that, the door was zipped wide open again and brighter dawn light filled the tent and made Josh's eyes squint shut. He held up a hand to block the light and watched through narrowed eyes as Devlin Stone climbed through the gap, turned around, winked, then zipped the tent door shut.

As he heard the man's footsteps passing through the grass, Josh's head sought the softness of his pillow. He rolled to his side and begged for this all to be an awful nightmare.

2

NIGHTMARE

Mind shut off, and laying on his back, the hard and painful throb of his heart lulled him to a distant place near sleep. He dozed, set himself adrift, paddling with the hope that this was all an illusion.

When he opened his eyes again, the pain had lessened. The day was brighter beyond the tent's nylon and there was the sound of voices outside now. He snorted, sat upright, grabbed at his neck again as fresh pain poked behind his eyes. First thing he did was look to where Kimmy should lay. The spot was still empty, and it pinged in his head immediately that truth worked against his hope the dream was really just that: a dream.

Now he fell forward onto both elbows, examined with one squinted eye where he'd imagined Devlin had been. Kimmy's sleeping bag was disturbed, but there was no obvious sign that jolted a recall to prove

Devlin had ever been there. What was he looking for, anyway?

"Ah, fuck," he groaned, and rubbed his face with one clawed hand. His breaths came hot and labored, his head throbbed. People were talking near the tent, but far enough he couldn't make out what they said. Someone laughed; further away, a guy shouted out for someone's attention. Face buried in his hands, he lingered, breathing through his fingers, gathering the strength to rise.

It had all been a dream. It just had to be. One: he wouldn't ask Devlin to sleep with his wife. What the fuck was that? Why would his brain conjure that story? Solely to torture himself, he figured. It was the stuff of nightmares. Devlin and Kimmy together was a wildly frightening thought. Two: even if he'd asked Devlin to sleep with Kimmy (seriously, get the fuck out of here with that shit), what the dream-Devlin had said would require Kimmy's acquiescence. *Not in a million years. Sorry, Devlin.* Unless he forced himself on Kimmy, pinned her down and (good Lord) raped her, the things dream-Devlin told him weren't true. If dream-Devlin turned out to be real, then real Devlin only sought to fuck with old Josh like this was still high school. And that made sense; doing something like tricking a guy into believing he'd asked Devlin to fuck his wife was right in Devlin's character.

Now he let out a satisfying groan, scratching nails over the back of his head, getting his neck tingling. It was ridiculous, and now, as he came more awake, the details of the dream began to grow foggy. Fucking weird though, dreaming of Devlin coming in and saying all that shit, and even weirder, dreaming of Devlin showing him his massive erection. What the hell was that all about? You could chalk it up to the high school reunion, he figured. Being in the old school halls and around those familiar faces conjuring up some of the more frightening ghosts of his past. And what was more striking than entering puberty, forced into naked shower proximity with bigger boys, seeing the bigger boys's bigger sexual organs, and them capitalizing on the revelation of your slower development. And Devlin was the epitome of the bully. And, yes, he had a big dick, fuck, everybody knew that—why he would dream of the guy hard like that was beyond him.

Bag unzipped, Josh slipped a leg out, and the movement showed him he was worse off than he thought. His temples pounded anew, his eyes blossomed faint white orbs; his stomach rolled over. "Oh fuck," he sighed. He was still drunk, too; he could feel it.

It was cold out of his sleeping bag, and he padded hands around, wincing and squinting, finding his sweatshirt and donning it. He pulled up the hood, located his jeans and put his legs in them, the whole while fighting with the queasy pounding effect of too much alcohol.

Now he was unzipping the tent, poking his head out into the morning. Campfire smoke hung heavy in the air. On his left, a fog hovered on the flat surface of the lake. Morning was still and quiet except for the sound of a single songbird. Dotted in disarray around the campfire were overturned lawn chairs and empty beer bottles and Solo cups. There, behind his SUV, was the picnic table where dream-Devlin had said the two of them chatted. Ridiculous. The two of them would never chat, even ten years removed from high school. And on that picnic table there were beer bottles and the bottle of whiskey he'd been drinking last night. It was empty. That was another truth.

He broke from a crouch, tried to stand, ended up hunching over with his hands thrust in the pouch of his sweatshirt; he lurched up the grassy hill toward the log cottage that looked out over Birch Lake.

Lights shone in the kitchen, and he could see through the windows people were awake and moving. He checked his watch. It was seven now. Probably two hours since he and dream-Devlin had their exchange in the tent.

There were familiar faces strewn on the lawn, people with similar hangovers, proffering timid waves his way, some holding heads, some looking like they were going to heave their guts in the toilet if they could just make it into the house. Someone hadn't even made it into the house or a tent. They lay on the grass, but some kind soul had put a pillow under their head and two blankets over top of them.

He mounted the back deck steps, leaned on the barbecue for a moment, looking into the house through the sliding glass doors. Devlin Stone stood in there talking to Amy (another person Josh hadn't seen since high school). Amy was telling Stone off about something. Arms folded across her chest, she scowled at him while he spoke. Stone's back was to Josh, so he couldn't see his face, but he pictured it as smug and uncaring.

Once he had the strength, he heaved off the barbecue, made it to the back door and slid it open. There were girls on the other side of the kitchen he hadn't seen because of the drapes—maybe a half dozen of them. Kimmy was one of them.

He was so glad to see her. But when she turned, she wasn't glad to see him—or at least didn't acknowledge seeing him. She was upset. Her black hair hung heavy around her pretty face, her brow was lowered as if in a scold, but her eyes had the glassy shine of a person upset; on the verge of crying, or already having cried. Her face looked puffy, her meager makeup cleared from her face, just her natural beauty —as pinched as it was in a mask of vex. She still wore her oversized cotton cardigan—one with deer and moose in a broad stripe around the torso—belted around her waist; she was swimming in it. Her narrow shoulders barely peeped out from its broad shawl collar.

When their eyes met, pain went through Kimmy's face, and her lips wriggled like she would cry. A girl she stood with registered Kimmy's reaction and looked his way over her shoulder. Another girl moved to console Kimmy, putting an arm around her.

His heart made a funny sag, then committed to sinking. Was it possible Stone was real, and he wasn't lying?

Josh made the dozen steps past the kitchen table, put his elbows on the island, asked his wife, "What's wrong? What's going on?"

"Nothing," the girl facing Kimmy said in a soothing tone, turning, putting up her placating hands, preventing Josh from coming around the island. "Nothing's wrong, Josh, nothing's wrong at all."

He asked his wife anyway: "Kimmy, what's wrong?"

The girls surrounded her protectively, and Kimmy's voice came from behind them, saying, "I'm fine, I'm fine." She'd dipped her head, and rubbed her brow with the heel of a hand.

One of the girls with Kimmy was her friend Karina. They'd stayed friends since high school, through college, and everafter. It was Karina's stupid idea to go to the reunion, and even worse, it was her idea to come to Tiffany's party, even though Kimmy expressed reservations. Karina was watching Josh, a look of worry on her face too, but when their eyes met, Karina mouthed: "It's okay, Josh."

He mouthed back: "Is it?" Karina nodded.

Karina and Kimmy shared the same beauty; Amy a Polish strawberry-blonde with a short bob, Kimmy a Taiwanese girl with a Betty Page haircut. Two slender, well-behaved girls who cared for each other; Karina rubbed Kimmy's shoulder while Kimmy still pressed hand-heel to forehead.

Josh turned, squinted against the light, watching Amy and Devlin talking still, Devlin casual, smug like he'd predicted, smiling. Amy still had important things to say, her posture showing some anger. Was this drama Devlin related or was this coincidental? No one else in the house seemed engaged in Kimmy's emotions, no one else seemed engaged in Devlin and Amy's kerfuffle. People lounged on couches, three girls (shit, women now, high school was a long time ago) sat in a circle on the floor cross-legged and going through their purses; Moe, from the soccer team, ate cereal from a bowl at the kitchen table. Most everyone oblivious to the living theater happening on two opposite sides of the house's main floor. Devlin and Kimmy could have two *separate* problems, couldn't they?

Josh looked back to Karina, mouthed, "What's going on?"

Karina shook her head, shrugged, turned up her nose. "Just girl stuff."

He looked back to Stone again, now with his arms crossed, big hands tucked in arm pits, head cocked. Still smiling. Shit, he was wearing sweatpants, shorts, and a black T-shirt, just like dream-Devlin. *Had he worn that last night?* No, he didn't think so. That was what the guy wore to crash in at bed time, it looked.

Had he seen Devlin wearing that? He must have—if he didn't, dream-Devlin was real. More likely, he'd seen Devlin wearing that outfit in his blackout drunk phase before he'd crashed in the tent (which he didn't even remember doing).

An anger returned now, and Josh rubbed his face. If there was one guy on earth who deserved to be taught a lesson, it was Devlin Stone. But who would teach it to him? Even though he was an adult now, it wouldn't be Josh. Stone still dangled power over everyone's head. He was taller, more muscular; physically, there wasn't anything Josh could do. Devlin inherited a management position at Stone Custom Brokerage LLC (go figure, how did you get that job, Devlin?), and made incredible money; what way was there to put Devlin in his place? But if something had occurred here between Kimmy and Devlin (not sex, Josh, come on already) and it was bad enough to upset Kimmy, shouldn't Josh stand up to the bully? Wouldn't he be compelled to march over there right now and confront the man? For Kimmy he would, despite the knowledge it wouldn't go well. The fear of humiliation swelled up from somewhere inside him where it had hidden deep for the last ten years since high school. That nausea returned, and he instantly knew he would soon throw up. His upper lip went sweaty, a prickly heat crawled his neck. Just the idea of going over to Devlin had him wilting and his balls retracting. Bourbon helpfully reminded him how weakened he was: *Don't do it, Josh, for God's sake, even if you were at your best, it would be an awful task. . . .* He wiped his mouth, looked away from Devlin and tried to push back the terrifying thought of confronting his high school bully in front of all these former classmates.

Karina crossed to his side, leaned on the island's counter, the two of them on their elbows facing each other. She asked him if he was all right.

"Mm," he moaned, rubbing his neck, "not feeling so good."

"You drank a lot."

He sighed, bile in his stomach rising, a lurching fear he may barf right in front of Karina and all over Tiffany's emerald tiled countertop—shit, how would he go to school on Monday? He chuckled to himself at the absurd thought, took long deep breaths to quell the noxious rising tide in his belly. The storm calmed, the queasiness appeased. With his eyes closed, he said to Karina, "What's going on with Devlin?" He jabbed a thumb over his shoulder, rolled with his ribs against the island's edge, craned his hurting neck to look at Amy and Stone again; the room swayed drunkenly. He burped, groaned.

Karina said, "It's no big deal, Josh."

Stone shrugged now, the motion exaggerated, his big shoulders up to his ears; he still showed Amy that arrogant expression. In a demanding tone, Amy said something, a firmer reiteration: "So just go, okay?"

Stone said, "I still don't know what the big deal is."

Amy said, "She wants you to."

Over his shoulder now, he saw Kimmy trying to get away from her clutch of friends, weaving around them with her arms folded; they prevented it, putting hands on her. "No, come on, hold on, guys," she said softly.

As she got nearer, Josh asked her again what was going on.

Kimmy looked his way, but not into his eyes, instead at his chest and stomach. "Nothing's wrong, Josh, it's nothing."

"Kimmy, something's wrong," he said, moving to meet her at the end of the island, putting out a shaky hand to stop her.

"I'm sorry," she said, "can you just give me a minute—just *one* minute."

"One minute for what?"

"I'm dealing with something, Josh."

"What's been going on?"

Karina said again, "It's just girl stuff, Josh. Just give her a minute." She rubbed Kimmy's shoulder.

The words were just placation, it was obvious— not *girl stuff* at all because now he watched as Kimmy left the kitchen to enter the family room, headed to where Devlin stood by the leather loveseat that backed onto the high cathedral window looking out to the lake. Whatever the problem was, it did involve Devlin and Kimmy. Amy saw Kimmy approach, crossed her arms, gave an uncomfortable smile to Kimmy and stepped backward.

Josh shook his head and closed his eyes. The *girl stuff* was between his wife and the guy who'd come into his dreams to tell him he'd fucked his wife. He watched intently, Amy entering the kitchen now, walking with her arms crossed, trying to avoid him, but he met her gaze and gave an expression that demanded answers. Amy came to the counter and leaned her back against it; he wanted to ask her what the fuck was going on, but watched his wife instead.

Kimmy got closer but kept her distance, Devlin watching her with restrained amusement. Kimmy had the same pose as all the women involved: arms crossed, mad, shocked maybe, shoulders slumped. All signs that while Josh had slept off a bottle of bourbon, something major had transpired. Kimmy still stood, her approach hesitant. She wore cut off jean shorts, but you couldn't see them under the long cardigan, so it looked like his wife was just standing there before Devlin in only a sweater, naked legs and bare feet.

Kimmy said something to Devlin they couldn't hear, and with her hair hanging down and blocking her face from this angle, Josh couldn't read her lips or her expression. Devlin nodded his head to the right. They disappeared from view, heading toward the fireplace like they need a more private place to talk.

Josh asked Amy what the fuck was going on, and Amy looked for an answer, her eyes going up and to the right, where everyone sought to find the most appropriate lie. She returned with, "I think they just had a fight."

"Just a fight?" He feared that it was far more than that. His hands tingled with dread. "What *happened* last night?"

Before she answered, he slid himself farther along the island so he could see where they went. Kimmy and Stone stood at the mantle, a crossing timber through stacked fieldstone twenty feet high. Amy joined him, her movements hesitant.

She said, "You went to bed. You had some help..."

"I was drunk."

"You were," Amy said, her voice slowing down as she sought time to manufacture a suitable story. "Yeah, you went to bed and a bunch of us stayed up. Things got, I guess, uh, heated."

"Is Kimmy okay?"

"She's totally fine. They just have to work something out."

"Kimmy and Devlin?"

Amy nodded. They watched Devlin and Kimmy now talking by the fireplace. Around him, Amy and Karina watched, the other girls, too. Two faces were familiar, two may have been wives of guys who went to Dalton. Had all of them witnessed this *heated* event?

He leaned to Amy. "Did Devlin *say* something to make her mad?"

"Yeah."

"What is it—is it really bad?"

Amy's mouth went to one side as she frowned. "She'll tell you. . . . Let Kimmy tell you."

"Well . . . do I need to *do* something?" *Like what, Josh, go fuck him up?*

"No, let her deal with it. Kimmy's a big girl."

Now he watched his wife standing close with Devlin Stone, who was a head taller than her. She looked small and slender next to his tall, lean build. Devlin put up a muscular arm on the timber mantle set in the stone fire place. They talked low, talked like two people settling something. Then whatever was needed to be said was done. Stone showed his palms, Kimmy shook her head no and rolled her eyes. Now she returned to them, padding bare feet silently across the polished maple floor littered with beer bottles. She came straight to him, and he received her with his open arms, a sudden relief and warmth flooding his heart. Kimmy lay her head in the hollow of his neck and he put his arms around her. He whispered, "Can you tell me what the hell is going on?"

"He's just such an asshole," she said.

"What did he say? Did he do anything?"

Kimmy rocked her head on his chest. "Can we just pack up and get the hell out of here, please?"

EVERYTHING WAS PACKED UP IN TWENTY MINUTES and loaded into their Qashgqai. Uncomfortable good-byes were said, uncaring hugs were given. The reunion had been fun, but he was looking forward to not seeing the majority of these people again for another decade. Devlin Stone was nowhere to be seen, but as they drove out Tiffany's tree-shaded gravel drive, they passed his black Mercedes roadster gleaming in the sun. Kimmy clucked her tongue when she saw it.

He said, "Are you ready to tell me what happened now?"

"No," she said.

He was in the passenger seat, head pounding, next to his wife, practically seeing double. He'd thrown up in the toilet in the middle of packing the tent, abandoning Kimmy to run into the house and get it done finally. It made him feel only marginally better. When he'd come back, Kimmy had taken the slack, kept working, the Nissan loaded with their gear and his wife looking to get the hell out of Harrowsmith.

Kimmy was behind the wheel in her big cardigan, Converse sneakers on now. He watched her bare legs on the leather seat because it was too bright to look out the window. He said, "Are you okay?"

"I am. Can I tell you about it some other time?"

"Just tell me what happened last night. With *me*."

Kimmy sighed, scratched her head, silver bangles singing on her skinny wrists. "Where do you remember up to?"

He hummed, head aching, stomach sloshing still, hugging his arms around himself. "I remember the barbecue, remember swimming. I remember drinking a lot of beer..."

"Then the whisky came out," she said, turning the Qashqai left onto a wider road, looking both ways, sitting more upright.

"Right..."

She got the Nissan up to speed, the roadway desolate and devoid of traffic. "Then, I don't know, we were all hanging around by the fire, everybody was just talking. You passed out..."

"Where?"

"I don't know, near the where the car was parked—"

"By the picnic table?"

"Yeah. . . . Amy and I helped you into the tent. . . . Actually you said you had to pee, and we took you in the bushes. I got your stuff off and I got you into your sleeping bag as best I could..."

"You helped me pee?" Another wave of dread came over him; how fucking embarrassing.

"You said you had to pee. I didn't want you to pee in your sleeping bag."

Shame rose up fast and he could feel his cheeks burning. How emasculating. So drunk his wife had to help him pee so he wouldn't wet the bed like a little boy. "God, I'm so sorry."

"It's fine, Josh. You know it's fine."

"What do you mean, you helped me pee?"

"What it sounds like," she said in a way that made him understand she *knew* how shameful his drunkenness was.

"Really?" Now he could assume she'd taken his

pants down or drew down his fly. Did she have to hold it for him? "Was Amy there?"

"We didn't want you to fall."

"So she was there."

"Don't worry, she wasn't looking."

"But she was *there?*" He buried his face in his hands and moaned into them. Amy had held him up so he wouldn't fall over, and his wife had held his dick to aim his pee. Jesus Christ. His stomach flinched with an awful thought. He croaked: "Was Devlin there too?"

Kimmy frowned. "Devlin? No."

"Fuck, I'm so sorry, Kimmy."

She patted his leg, and it made him jump. His eyes popped open to see her hand on him. "It's okay, baby."

"It's so embarrassing."

Both hands on the wheel, she said, "Don't worry. *Everyone* was in the bag. You didn't embarrass yourself. I don't think anyone saw. . . . I got you to bed."

"No one saw except you and Amy."

"She loves you."

No, she didn't. He groaned again, unable to shake this tangible *physical* feeling of awesome regret. *Why did he drink so much?*

He said, "And you stayed up?"

"Yeah."

It occurred to him she'd maybe never gone to bed. "Where did you sleep?" *Don't say the tent because I know you weren't there, Kimmy, if you say the tent you're a liar and Devlin Stone fucked you.*

"I *didn't* sleep," she said, not a brag or a proclamation; Kimmy's own regret and shame dripped from her words.

He bit his lip, rolled his head her way. "What did you do all night?"

Her mouth made an awkward movement, and he didn't like the beat it took her to answer. "We were up talking."

"You and Devlin?"

She looked his way, troubled. "No, Josh. Devlin was up, yeah . . . Me and Amy and some of the others. . . . Not everybody crashed."

Kimmy barely drank. It wasn't in her culture. Her dad was a hardcore Christian. "But Devlin was up with you guys?"

"He was around."

"Well, he must have been around. . . . And you must have been talking for you guys to get in a fight."

Kimmy's jaw clenched. She grimaced, shook her head. A hand came up again to shake through her hair, bangles singing. "Can we just drop it? For now, Josh."

It was all too much for him to endure, anyway. His body pulsed with pain. The bourbon still punished him. His mind throbbed, his thoughts were poisoned by a man that came to him in a dream. Right now, it was clear everything pointed to Kimmy messing around with Devlin. Devlin's visit was real. It wasn't a dream. The only thing that made him think Kimmy had fucked Devlin was because Devlin had come into the tent to tell him that. Devlin and Kimmy got in a fight. Kimmy was no dummy. She might not be a VP of some billion-dollar shipping brokerage, but she was a lawyer even if she wasn't working right now. A spot she'd earned, not been gifted. Kimmy had smoked Devlin in some argument and Devlin said something nasty that hurt her feelings. Then that wicked asshole knew how to get back at her in the profoundest way possible: fuck with her husband's head—her husband, who he already abused and tormented since they were young. Maybe there was more to it, but right now, logic was insurmountable. His body wanted to hibernate and his brain literally wanted to die. Trying to think his way out of this was like swimming in a straight jacket. One thing he knew: had he not been visited by Devlin and Devlin's huge erection in the middle of the night and instead woken fresh and untainted to the drama playing out in Tiffany's cottage this morning, the last thing he would have thought was his wife had cheated on him.

"Whatever," he said. "It's okay, Kimmy."

He ducked his head down, and Kimmy turned on the radio, tuned it to BBC news. They came to a stop, and he looked around, the world around him swimming and uneven. The intersection was a five-way in a very small town; red brick buildings, white clapboard homes. Kimmy sighed. "Where the fuck?" She leaned close to the windshield, trying to read the road signs. No other traffic rushed them, they were the only car. She tapped the Nissan's display menu, got it to navigation, tapped again for the route home. She pointed out the window to a road that led sixty degrees south, saying to herself, "I guess it's that one," because he was of no help to her now. The car rolled through the intersection and now the nav showed they were on the right path, the car's woman voice saying they would arrive home in one hour and fifty-nine minutes.

He rubbed his neck; Kimmy reached behind them between the seats, pulled through the gap a pillow and passed it to him. "Put that under your head," she said.

"I have such a headache."

"You took Tylenol?"

"I took a ton of Tylenol," he said. "Moe had some."

"You hungry—you want to stop soon, grab something to eat? I bet there's a Timmy's in Odessa."

"Maybe in an hour," he said, nestled his head in the pillow and closed his eyes.

3
AJAX

osh passing out in the car was a blessing she didn't deserve. *The horrible, detestable thing she'd done to the man she loved.*

With Josh comatose next to her, she was able to cry. Off and on, and when the tears came, she cried as quietly as she was able next to her husband. It was a battle the whole way back to Ajax.

Why had they gone to the stupid reunion?

She didn't even *want* to go. It was Karina who'd convinced her, Karina saying Amy would be there, and they hadn't been in Amy's company a long time— almost ten years. Did she really need to catch up on what *everyone* from Dalton had been doing since graduating? No, she didn't. They should have attended the reunion at the most, stayed at a hotel and met up for one more visit with Amy today before she headed back to London. Go to a restaurant and have a meal like normal twenty-eight-year olds, not some lakeside rager like they were still a bunch of kids.

And *certainly* not spend time with Devlin Stone. Fucking Devlin Stone. . . . Just the interior mention of his name had her palms beating up and down in quiet anger on the steering wheel—not too loud because she didn't want to wake up Josh. Devlin fucking Stone.

The reunion party at Dalton had been fine. It was a blast to be with Amy again. Since Amy had gone to Scotland for university, they'd fallen out of touch because of the distance. The occasional email was about it these days since Amy had moved to London after graduating with an MBA. But it was Amy's idea to go to Tiffany's cottage party. Though Karina and Josh were just as guilty. Amy and Tiffany had been pretty good friends back in high school, though their friendship was a lot of wishful thinking on Amy's part, in her opinion. Tiffany only hung with girls whose parents drove BMW or Mercedes. Tiff hung with Amy because Amy was pretty and kind of cool, but mostly because Amy tutored Tiff in math. Their friendship wasn't exactly one for the ages, as they say, and she doubted they ever did more than comment on each other's Facebook posts since college.

Since she wasn't a drinker, they should have just gone to the reunion function, ate the dinner, and skipped the house party. Who would have anticipated it would be so wild, and that these people ten years removed from high school would revert to juvenile drinking games and dumbass shenanigans? Why did grown-ups think they could drink so much? Fucking Josh. Why did he drink? Leaving her all alone all night with a bunch of drunk people.

Devlin Stone wasn't drunk either.

Now she beat on the wheel again. No, Devlin Stone liked to be in control. Devlin Stone didn't like to have his wits dampened by spirit. *He told you that— whether you wanted to know about it or not.* Devlin Stone loved his philosophies. Loved how those philosophies delivered success. Piece of privileged shit starting off life on third base, now acting like it was all his philosophies that led to the great wonder and spectacle of the fabulous life he was living. Not fucking likely. She fucking hated Devlin Stone. Fucking A-1 hated him all through high school. Never thought of him once in college. Never thought of him after college. Never thought of them since she was married.

Then how did this happen, Kimmy?

Amy and Karina were impressed, goggling like a bunch of teenagers. Impressed by his business travel, his adventure travel . . . all the show-off shit she figured her cynical friends would see through, especially so far removed from high school. The fact any of them knew Devlin'd just bought a two-million dollar house was a sign Devlin Stone was a bigmouth bastard. Dropping prices on everyone so they knew how much money he must be making. How could anyone fall for that—be *impressed* by that gross display? God, but she wasn't.

How she ended up in this predicament she would never figure out. But she was hip deep, and that was for sure.

Josh still slept when they pulled into the parking lot of their apartment building, and she considered not rousing him, maybe just cracking a window open and slipping inside. They were on the second floor and the balcony looked down over the vehicle. She would just let him sleep, let him have this peace, keep an eye on him. But what would the neighbors think, seeing her husband asleep midday Sunday in the passenger seat of their car? *Oh, look who has a drinking problem.*

With reluctance, she shook Josh's arm. When he came to, she stroked his cheek. "How are you feeling?"

He made to answer, but his lips stuck together. She thumbed his earlobe but couldn't look in his eyes; instead, she watched for his lips to move.

"Mm, mm-okay," he said.

"We're home," she told him.

A look of happiness lightened his face. "We are?"

"You slept the whole way, baby."

"Good," he said, and rubbed at his forehead.

"Headache?"

"Tylenol worked," he said. "Mm, but my back's

sore." He sat up now, unclipping his seatbelt, his features pinched in pain, eyes squinted against the light.

"Why don't you go inside? I'll get the bags."

"No, I'll get them."

She rubbed his shoulder, saying, "Baby, just go inside and have a nap. Let me get the things in. There's not much; two trips tops." He nodded, leaned toward her like a kid, and she kissed his hairline. "Go on upstairs," she whispered.

She watched her husband lumber out of their vehicle, slam shut the door, then shuffle across the parking lot; she fought more tears. Devlin fucking Stone. That good-looking loudmouth piece of shit, him and all his stupid football buddies, him and all those cheerleader sluts. Most of those girls made her life miserable. *How did she end up like this?*

The tears came, and she let them, now she was alone. She covered her face in her hands so the neighbors wouldn't see. A drunk husband sleeping it off in the car was bad, and a crying wife was no better. Fucking gossip factory, this damn building. So she sniffed, snatched napkins out of the glove compartment to dry her eyes and blow her nose.

It took two trips like she'd said, and she unloaded the car by herself, not seeing Josh once, knowing he'd slipped into the bedroom to catch some more Zs.

When she was settled, she went to the bathroom and stripped off what she wore. Stupid cardigan, her tight jean shorts. *Had she given off signals?*

Sure, the cardigan covered it all, but were her jeans too short?

Why would she blame herself for this?

Because of what you did...

Oh, yeah, right. But she didn't lure him in, she didn't...

Her hands were shaking when she opened the mirrored vanity and brought out the digital thermometer. She greased the tip with petroleum jelly, stripped off her panties and put the thermometer in her rectum. It was an uncomfortable and awkward moment, just her and her reflection. She looked into her own eyes, shaking her head, standing on her tiptoes, one hand on the sink, one shoulder cranked back with her hand holding the thermometer situated in her rectum.

"Please, please, please, oh, please..."

The monitor beeped. She pushed with her stomach, tugged and winced, took a deep breath in preparation then looked at the readout.

"Shit." Almost ninety-nine degrees.

There was a good chance she was ovulating.

The thermometer bounced and clattered in the sink and she threw herself down to sit her bare ass on the toilet seat and cried into her hands, gulping and choking back her sounds so she wouldn't alert Josh to what she'd done.

·   ·   ·

THE GUEST ROOM OF THEIR APARTMENT WAS HER workspace. She was the figurehead of the sole proprietorship, commonly doing business as Katt Basket. And, yes, most people online thought her name was Katt Basket. *Hi, nice to meet you, I'm Katherine, yes, Katherine Basket, that's right.*

She'd been pregnant last year and taken time off work. The pregnancy turned out a no-go. In the meantime, she'd been puttering around, had this idea for an Etsy store. Granny Chang had been a masterful basket weaver, and when she was little and would spend some weekends with her grandmother, they would bake, watch soap operas, and weave baskets. Granny Chang immigrated from Taiwan to Canada when she was first married, and had grown up in a Beitou mountain village, learning homemaking skills like rush-weaving. So young Kimmy had earned some mad weaving skills, though not as advanced as her mother's mother. Enough, she could weave out a large basket a day, throw a snappy oblong cushion inside, and sell it online as a cat bed for twenty or so over two-hundred dollars, depending. It was just fun at first, but then her shop took off and she was doing a basket a day for weeks in a row, five days a week, maybe a little extra on the weekend if Josh was out with his buddies. Ahead of her were seventy-eight orders, and more came in regularly, one every other day, then sometimes four in a day. It was nice to be at home, but her hands were sore these days and she could hide in the apartment and pretend that was okay, but soon she knew she'd have to get back to work at her real job. Or get pregnant again, if she could.

She set the bundled grass down and stared across the room. Even busywork couldn't settle her mind. Her mouth slimmed, and she felt a tremble in her jaw.

That opinionated piece of shit.

The audacity . . . and the mouth on him.

One second they're arguing, she's raising her voice, he's sneering; he had her so riled she wanted to claw his face. She put up a hand—not to lay it on him in any way but just to signify how close she was to throttling him. He grabbed her wrist. When she pulled it away, he didn't let go. They struggled. She brought up the other hand to swat at him. He'd grabbed that one too. Both her hands in his control, he kissed her fully on the mouth. She'd tried to knee him, tried to elbow him, but he put his weight against her. Her heart had pounded with rage, but the fight in her diverted . . . and it was all so unexpected.

* * *

KIMMY WAS IN HER STUDIO MAKING BASKETS, HE figured, because he heard her music. He was face down in bed, eyes closed. He took inventory. Neck and shoulders a little stiff. Throbbing headache gone, pounding white sheets that had been flashing behind his eyes also gone. Nausea zero. He did, however, feel like he'd been run over by a Mack truck. Another item in his inventory: an erection throbbing at 110%. He squeezed his hips, pushed it into the mattress. Pee boner. He had to get to the can.

He drew in a long breath, happy when his mind and stomach didn't do a somersault. The hangover had passed. It was 7:22, according to the bedside clock. He'd slept for nine hours, right through the worst of his bourbon punishment. Thank God. But soon, the shameful feelings of regret began to wash over him. What had he said last night? What had he done? And... "Oh, fuck. Right."

His stomach sank.

That whole thing with Devlin.

He'd slept through the day and missed all that hurt, but now it was ready and waiting for him, one leg crossed over the other, sitting at the foot of his bed holding a pistol like a Bond villain ready to torment him.

He groaned, rolled over, the sudden humiliation slapping him cold in the face. All those things that Devlin had said. How he'd had sex with Kimmy. It was ludicrous, though. There was no way on earth he could be telling the truth. Devlin was fucking with him. God damn ten years out of high school and that piece of shit still thought it was funny to fuck with some easygoing 'lesser' guy. Once an asshole, always an asshole. There was just no way what Devlin had said was true. Kimmy hated Devlin and all those guys all through high school. Kimmy was smart. She spoke four languages; before her mat leave she was an immigration lawyer. She didn't fall for shit. She was cynical and tough, with a heart of gold.

Now he was kind of mad. Just the fact that Devlin would make a joke like that—make a joke he'd put his hands on Kimmy, let alone put his penis inside her. The thought tightened his stomach into a hard node of anger.

"Motherfucker," he said to the quiet room. Kimmy got in a fight with Devlin. That was it. Politics, for sure. You could see that one a mile away. So things got a little heated, things were said. . . . That made sense. Kimmy must've got the better of Devlin, and that snide privileged fuck slipped into the tent to poison her husband's mind and turn him against her. There was no way he'd asked Devlin to sleep with Kimmy. It had never even occurred to him. Why would he ask for that?

A worry began to tighten him. It was possible that Devlin had also worked some insinuation into Kimmy, or maybe Kimmy's friends. Taking advantage of their fight, cupping his hand and whispering into everyone else's ears. What if he told other people that Josh asked him to fuck Kimmy?

Shame reddened his cheeks. The girls at the party surrounding Kimmy this morning, ameliorating, telling him it was just girl stuff and not to worry. . . . Had Devlin told them Josh asked him to sleep with Kimmy—was that the cause of the kerfuffle? Did Devlin whisper that nonsense in Kimmy's ear? Amy's?

"Just girl stuff, Josh." Amy was dismissive, and that would be exactly what she'd say to him in the wake of some shocking blow-out. . . . Could that be what Kimmy fought with Devlin over? Devlin laying a move on her saying Josh wanted him to, and that's how the fight started? . . . But he had to consider the possibility, however remote, that the lie worked on Kimmy and she'd said, *Well, okay, if Josh insists*. He groaned and chuckled at the idea. Too crazy. Not Kimmy, no way.

Both hands covered his stomach. It growled. He was starving. His right hand lowered, slipped under his briefs, thumb-jabbed the topside of his erection and pushed it downward, tenting out the front of his underwear.

Now he pictured being drunk last night, Amy and Kimmy helping him to the tent, stopping for a pee break. Kimmy fishing his dick out and it was hard like this. Unsteady on his feet, Amy supported him, and being a girl and having girl curiosities, even knowing she shouldn't, she took a peep while Kimmy managed his pee stream. This is what Amy saw. He peeled back the front of his shorts and looked at what he had. Not bad. No complaints. The idea of Amy taking a peep was so fucking arousing his muscles tightened, his cock throbbing harder with the prospect of being spied by another girl.

But there were better-equipped men like Devlin Stone out there. When Devlin had pushed out the front of his sweatpants to fan what he claimed was

Kimmy's sex smell off of his genitals, Josh looked. Other girls, a lot of girls from his high school, had been with that. The thing looked to be twice the size of his own (but that was an illusion. It *couldn't* be twice the size). How does one guy get born into money with a face like that, a body like that, and a dick like that? If Josh had been born into it, he was sure he wouldn't be the toxic piece of shit Devlin was. Imagine being with Kimmy and you had all that. . . . Imagine being with Kimmy and you had a couple of nice cars in the driveway of your couple-million dollar house. You made money, everybody was nice to you, wanted to be your friend (or at least kissed your ass), and when you got your sweet Kimmy in bed at night, she couldn't wait to get on her back and open her legs for your huge cock.

The front of his underwear was pushed down his thighs to expose his naked arousal. Still held upright, he examined it. Maybe half of what Devlin had in total volume—Devlin was thicker and many inches longer. His other hand faffed around on the bed, reached for the night table and retrieved his phone. He pushed it against the dorsal side of his rock hard erection. Not much longer than an iPhone. It was possible Devlin could be two iPhones.

He squeezed his thighs together, wondering what it would be like to have that, show it to Kimmy, lay her down and put it inside her.

His hand teased, stroked; he closed his eyes. Now he was thinking about walking in on that fight in the kitchen. Amy saying Hey, you know what, just let Kimmy and Devlin work it out. . . . What if when Devlin lied to Kimmy about her husband's request, he'd done the same thing he'd done to Josh, exposed his wicked arousal to her? What would Kimmy do seeing that monstrous thing? He humped his hand, hating this line of thinking despite the wildness shivering through him while he masturbated. The thought of his wife enraged but turned on hurt his stomach in an unexpected way.

What if Devlin wasn't kidding when he'd said he'd fucked her, and he'd been with Kimmy as Amy walked in? . . . In the bathroom, Kimmy up on the counter, Devlin trying to put that huge cock inside her and Amy walks in...

It was ludicrous, but he pictured it anyway. Kimmy's face as that thing went inside her. . . . Amy witnessing that...

The hardness in his bladder lessened as his penis began to consider a new function. Urination was put on the back burner despite its urgency, and now he was steadily jerking himself under the covers, freight-training to an orgasm. He tried to picture in his hand was what Devlin had, and his hand was Kimmy's tight insides as it pushed in and out of her, and Kimmy gasped and cried with pleasure...

"Shit, mm, shit," he hissed as he came, squeezing himself, thighs pressed together, grunting and bucking and trying to preserve the bedsheets from being dirtied.

The unexpected session left him gasping in the sheets, bewildered by the dark fantasy that had tickled him. Fucking Devlin Stone. In his tent this morning, not a dream, but a reality. A devil full of lies, and now his poison worked through his victim's bloodstream.

Then he was hunched over, quick-stepping to their bathroom, cleaning off his hands, wiping himself down, escaping the guilt of what he'd just imagined.

That was wild. Why would that be arousing? And if you thought it was arousing now, was it even the tiniest bit possible while loaded on bourbon he could have presented this idea to perhaps one of the guys he most hated in his entire life? He looked at his reflection in the mirror, the bags under his eyes, the heaviness in his expression. Eyes dipped down, he looked at his meager arousal poked out between his legs, fading from 100% down to 75, and feeling very inadequate. You couldn't even get her pregnant right.

Shower taps on hot, lever yanked over, he stepped under the shower's spray.

* * *

WHAT ON EARTH WAS SO AROUSING ABOUT RUINING her life? Here she was, back in the bathroom again wearing only a T-shirt, naked from the waist down, sitting on the toilet, calves flexing, feet bent up onto tiptoes, fast but gentle-jacking on her clit. She squinted her eyes, grimaced at the pleasure. Her pussy was alive right now, every touch she delivered racing through her system like greasy electricity.

The toilet tank's lid clunked and rattled as she humped her own hand, probing two bound fingers inside herself, feeling the slosh of her excitement, the dew in her tangled pelt. Then she gasped a shocked sound as the two fingers mashed on the swollen bulb of her clit again. Her feet cramped; her thighs shook; her ass muscles seized like cables.

"Oh, oh, oh," she whimpered, hoping the sound was subdued by the humming bathroom fan. Pipes in the wall hummed behind her; Josh was awake, getting into the shower.

Hand slapped over her mouth to stifle her crying, she orgasmed. Her two middle fingers zipped in a blur over her clit, shoulder muscles cramping, tricep muscles bulging, stomach tightened like a cord as the orgasm went on and on.

And when it was done, it left her sobbing again.

"What is wrong with me?" she cried into her hands. "Why, *why* did I do that?"

That was the real question. She hated Devlin Stone. Everyone knew it. Now she cried harder, thinking of Josh's broken heart. It would come out. This wasn't a secret. The drive home to Ajax had been her march to the electric chair. Electric truth was going to light up her body soon. Four people knew. By tomorrow, what would that number be?

4

BLANK SLATE

Once he was dressed in a soft, comfortable sweatshirt and sweatpants, he shuffled out into the hall and was instantly blessed with the smell of delicious food. His stomach tightened, and his throat gurgled. He smiled, though, coming to Kimmy's open doorway. She was in her Katt Basket room, in her glory really, laptop open, playing some Korean soap opera, hair tied up on the top of her head, sitting on her stool and weaving. She knew she was being watched, swiveled her stool a quarter turn to look over her shoulder at him.

"I heard you in the shower," she said. "How are you feeling?"

Her honest smile warmed him, instantly spritzing him like a garden hose and washing away all those nasty thoughts of her falling for Devlin Stone's bullshit. His knees dipped with happiness, and he smiled. "Feeling *so* much better."

"You hungry?"

"What the hell are you cooking? Is it bao?"

"I figured you'd be hungry, sleeping all day."

"I'm so starving, Kimmy," he said, laying a hand over his stomach.

"I waited for you. You're lucky you got up because I was about at my end—I'm hungry too, you know. I might've eaten yours while you slept."

He waited as she shut her studio down, and they walked to the kitchen together. From the warming oven, she withdrew a covered baking tray. He fell against the counter island that separated the living area from the kitchen, admiring her as she pulled back the tinfoil sheet. In the pan were four Gua Bao, or what Kimmy called Tiger Bites Pig, because the steamed bread that wrapped the stewed beef looked like a mouth chomping down. Her grandma made them with pork, but he preferred his with stewed beef, and so did Kimmy.

Two plates were served, and he popped the top on a plastic bottle of fizzy Coca-Cola for the sake of his hangover, and they ate together in front of the TV. When they were done, he collected their plates, washed them in the sink, wrapped up the remains and refrigerated them. It was 8:30 now, and he rejoined her on the couch, settling in next to her, hooking a leg behind her so she could rest her back against his stomach and chest. She fell against him and moaned. He said in her ear, "You're the best."

"Thank you," she said.

"Did I embarrass you last night?"

"No. You were fine," she said, stroking his hand. "Nobody could understand what you were saying, so you're okay."

"Good, my horrid racism is still a secret."

"You keep fooling them. Who would ever guess?"

"Score one for the bad guys," he said.

She laughed and wriggled her body against his.

"Sorry, though, you know, that I got so drunk."

"Don't worry about it. It's not like you have a *problem*."

"It's that frigging bourbon."

"You weren't the only one."

"Who else?"

"Adam and his brother . . . what's his name—"

"Cody."

"Yeah, the two of them drank a lot, too. They went skinny dipping in the water, like two in the morning."

"Really? They didn't have a heart attack?"

"Jacob was there. He's a paramedic."

"Nobody tried to stop them?"

"Everybody told them it wasn't a good idea."

"You watched them run into the water?" He wondered if they were naked and Kimmy saw.

"No, didn't want to be party to their deaths."

"That's a good plan. Fewer days in court."

Kimmy put up a hand for a high five and he gently palmed against her.

She asked, "What do you want to watch next?"

"Whatever you want," he said, then: "Hey, Kimmy...?"

"What?" she said, leaning forward to grab the remote.

"What was your fight with Devlin about?"

She paused, peeked over her shoulder at him. Her head went heavy to one side. She picked up the remote. "What do you think?"

"Politics," he said as she lay back against him again.

She said, "He is such a fucking asshole."

"Once an asshole, always an asshole."

"It's so true," she muttered, flicking through the menu on screen.

"His dad was an asshole, too."

"Never met the man," she said, "but I'm not surprised."

"That's all it was about?"

She said, "Yeah—what else?"

"I don't know—it seemed pretty serious."

She seemed to stiffen a little, but then softened. Her head tilted to rest against his shoulder, her temple touching the back side of the leather couch. She was quiet and serious when she spoke, saying, "It got heated. Wasn't just that we were disagreeing, we didn't handle it well. Things were said..."

"What did you say?"

"I'd rather not say."

"Oh. You telling me you're racist now too?"

"Shut up," she said and elbowed him. She began flicking through channels.

"So that's all it was?" he asked.

"Yeah. Look, I don't know what to tell you."

"Well, tell me the truth."

She breathed against him, taking her time. "People are going to say crazy things, you know."

"Yeah, no, I know. . . . Crazy how?"

"We fought a little."

"Yeah, you said that."

"No, I mean *fought*. Like with our hands."

"Did you punch him?" he said, incredulous.

"No. But we were . . . we were really mad," she said.

"Wait a second. Did he put his hands on you?"

"Yeah, but—"

"That fucking . . . we should call the cops."

"Not like that. Come on, don't . . . I just want this to be in the past already."

"Did he hurt you?"

"No, he was . . . look, I don't know," she said. "We both got physical, grabbing each other. I wanted to . . . I wanted to scratch his eyes out, you know? I *wanted* to punch him. I wanted to—I've never been so mad."

"That's not like you."

"I know. That's why I just want to forget about it."

"That's all that happened?" he said, and gripped the space between her shoulder and neck and gently massaged his thumb into her muscle. She tilted her head toward him, lay back against him.

"Can we just forget about it, Josh, please?"

"Yes, my pleasure," he said. "So people saw you fight?"

"I said can we forget about it."

"Sorry," he said. "Yes, we can forget about it."

Despite sleeping all day, he managed to drift off while they watched television. When he woke, his neck had a kink in it and Kimmy was standing, stretching, pointing the remote at the TV and turning it off. She dropped it to the table, turned to face him. He blinked, rubbed his neck, sat up straighter. She watched him, a look of concern on her face, worrying a tooth over the corner of her bottom lip. The light from the kitchen gently bathed on her front side, the family room dark now. She was a slim and innocent figure, cotton shrouded, and she belonged to him. She rubbed one hand up and down the opposite forearm, then held it out for him. She said, "Can you come to bed with me?"

He nodded, took her hand. They passed through the kitchen, making it dark, made their way down the hall to the bedroom.

With her hands on his chest, she guided him back toward the bed and made him sit. She stood above him, the dark and cloudy night beyond the windows, full dark, just her silhouette traced by the streetlights's pale amber glow. The room was deathly still, the soft sounds of her body moving against his loud in his ears. She put a knee on his thigh and cupped his neck, lowered her lips to his. He kissed her, closed his eyes and breathed her in. She was warm and loving. He held her waist, and she got both knees now on either side of his thighs and sat in his lap. He stroked her body, going from her waist, up her back, and over her shoulders while they made out, moving slowly, breathing deep. He sucked her tongue, bit her lip, let their kiss break apart so he could look in her eyes. He said, "You're so eager tonight."

She said nothing, but nodded. She kissed him again, and he held her, Kimmy beginning to sway her hips in his lap. He grew to full hardness, a frightening thought lurking in the dark, teasing him. Why's she so horny? Sure, she didn't cheat, she would never do that . . . But what got her so turned on? The way her husband got drunk and abandoned her at the party, embarrassed her, went unconscious in their tent? Did that get a girl super wet? No. Was it the way she had to drive home, and he slept? Then he stumbled and lurched into bed and continued another eight hour do-nothing marathon? Was that Kimmy's turn on? Was that the secret?

That was not the secret.

Now he pushed his hardness against her, squeezing his ass muscles and hugging her, pushing down with his hands on her neck and shoulders to hold her in place so he could hump himself against her panties.

It was hard right now to ignore the story of Kimmy and Devlin at the party—the way she hated Devlin, and the way she fought with him . . . Hate wasn't the opposite of love. Hate was akin. Hate was passion, like love was passion. Kimmy hated Devlin. Their fight had riled her. Their fight had been a surrogate for fucking. His wife had her engines fired up all day, waiting for the only man she was allowed to sleep with to be available, rested and healed. Well, he could do that. He *wanted* to do that.

Fuck, though, what if there was truth to what Devlin had told him? What if he'd said something like that to Devlin when he was drunk? No, Devlin was using it against him. Using it to hurt him. He had to stop letting that doubt creep inside him.

Kimmy went up higher on her knees, changing the lever of her fulcrum, her body weight resting against his and sending them both back onto the bed, mouths locked. She was over him, on top of him, on knees and elbows, kissing his mouth and kissing his neck while he caressed her body. He whispered, "I love you."

"I love you so much, Josh," she said in return, then kissed his lips again. Her hand went down, grabbed his hardness over his sweatpants. He presented it to her, proud to show her effect on him. She made a satisfied exhale, shifted her weight, began to push down his pants. His hands joined in, helping her, and they shimmied them down as she backed off the bed.

Now he watched her in the dim light, her cottony top off and away. She was beautiful, her lean but soft body undulating against the streetlights' glow. She pushed her pants down, stepped out of them, climbed on top of him again, and he lay back with her. They kissed, but Kimmy was still eager for sex. And now it was all he could focus on. No foreplay tonight. She didn't want him to use her mouth, didn't want his fingers. . . . She wanted cock. They usually played around a little, but tonight, he worried, it was another man who had her hungry for sexual penetration. She fumbled with his dick, angled it, lowered herself, swiping his tip against her hot, luscious seams, finding her opening and easing backward. His eyes rolled up and back as he felt himself sink into her oily velvet interior. She made no sound. No moan, no gasp. Now he wondered what a woman said when a man with what Devlin had went inside her. His pulse thundered at the thought, stomach going watery at the notion that Kimmy had perhaps seen Devlin's bulge, or heard the rumors. Of course she'd heard the rumors though—everyone knew he was hung. So, she got in a fight with a guy she hated, they grabbed at each other, she knew he was well endowed . . . She gets home . . . She wants it . . . Her husband doesn't have it.

She pushed her hips toward his feet and got his erection fully inside her. "Oh Kimmy," he sighed, rubbed the small of her back, then cupped her ass. But when all his forefront mind could think about was what Devlin had revealed to him in the tent, the wonderment of Kimmy taking something like that had worry wringing out his ecstasy. His brow grew troubled, and the more he hoped to maintain hardness, the more it escaped him. She worked up and down, and he tightened his ass muscles, hoping that would flex his diminishing arousal. But it was too late now. Kimmy was reaching behind—and he imagined she was checking to see if he was in. If she fucked Devlin, she would know he was in. But why would he even think that or consider it? She *hadn't* been with Devlin. Kimmy was never that kind of girl . . . "Sorry," he whispered.

"It's okay," she said, starting to hump him again, but now hardness had escaped him.

"Give me a second," he said as she rose, put a hip down next to him, and sat at his side. He went to pleasure himself but she beat him to it, her hand taking him in three fingers and a thumb, his thing wriggling around in her grip, slick from her excitement. Excitement he couldn't measure up to. Shit, what the fuck?—now *that* was making them hard. He grew again, grew in her hand.

"There we are," she said, "it's okay, see . . ."

"I'm still recovering," he told her, hoping that was it. Worrying it wasn't.

"It's okay," she said, "take your time . . ."

"You want me on top?"

"What do you want?" he asked, and then tried to picture Devlin asking what Kimmy wanted. He squinted, grimaced.

"You okay?" she whispered.

"Fine," he said, then: "I want to be on top."

Kimmy whispered that was good and scooted up past him to put her head in the pillows, laying on her back in their bed. He got on his knees, still stroking himself. Kimmy lay on the bed, naked, perfect. Her knees together, she slunk her legs, then lowered them and opened them. In the dim, he could see the black thatch of her love nest, that hot woman part of her, and tried to picture her this way, so beautiful and pure, through Devlin's eyes. Devlin the predator, Kimmy the prey. Laying back naked, reluctant . . .

He got over his wife, kissed her again, put a hand between them and guided his hardness inside her. Again, no sound from Kimmy, just breathing through her nose as their tongues wound together. Her forearms crossed the back of his neck, and he pushed himself in and out of her. "Love you so much," he gasped around their kissing. She hummed an affirmative sound in her throat. But, again, now all he could think of was how a man like Devlin would drive Kimmy wild. The sounds she would make if Devlin was over top of her, going into her.

"It's okay," she whispered, and that was when he realized the hardness of his arousal had dwindled again. Not raging hard and not halfway; somewhere in between. If Devlin were at the three-quarters erect, Kimmy would know he was in. Kimmy would have something still to work with. . . . Now what he had dwindled; decreased further.

"It's all right, Josh," she said, guided him out of her, gripped the back of his neck and pumped her fist on his flopping penis until he was fully hard again.

"I'm ready," he told her, but she whispered it was okay and kept her hand pumping up and down on him, stroking his neck, scratching her nails in the back of his hair and kissing him.

"It's okay," she said again, then gave him her tongue.

Hot pleasure burned in the center of his mind, right at the forefront behind his third eye, all focus on the intense pleasure of her rapidly moving hand. They kissed, and he listened to the slick patter of her jerking grip. "Josh," she whispered, "I want you to come."

"No," he said, "I'm good, I can go..."

"I just want you to come," she said again.

"Kimmy..."

"Tell me when you're ready . . . promise."

"Uh-huh," he grunted, the pleasure high and intense enough his brain began making deals: it's okay, come and then you can go down on her.

As the pressure built, he grunted more urgently: "Yeah, yeah, mm, I'm, mm, gonna..."

"Okay, inside, inside me," she said, hushed and rushed and urgently whispering.

"What?—inside..."

"Put it inside," she said, bucking her hips toward him.

He thumbed his erection downward, pushed inside Kimmy's slick interior; he humped, fast and hard, mattress squeaking, but in ten seconds he was boiling over, pulsing a weak but pleasurable load inside her. He'd already gone once today, jerking off in bed when he woke, and his body had better things to do today than replace dumb sexual fluids—it was just trying to survive a wicked hangover.

He grunted and snorted, hooked arms behind her, grabbed her shoulders and bit the pillow, thrust deep and ejaculated inside his wife.

"That's it," she said calmly, "okay, I love you," and stroked his back, teasing him, running her nails on his shoulder blades, which he loved.

When he was done, left panting, he withdrew, eased himself off of her, lay at her side searching for her hand. But Kimmy drew her knees up, grabbed her own shins, shoved a pillow under her butt. He knew the pose. They'd done this a lot last year when they were trying to conceive.

He stared at her and she watched him blankly, him waiting for her to explain herself. When she was quiet too long, he said, "We're trying again?"

She cupped a palm to his cheek, saying, "I think I'm ready."

* * *

IN THE MORNING LIGHT, KIMMY PACKED JOSH'S lunch—two turkey sandwiches on white, an extra pickle, an apple and a granola bar—while Josh got dressed for work in the bedroom. Everything into Josh's lunch bag, she zipped it closed and set it on the pass-through's counter so Josh could grab it as he walked to the front door.

A year ago, she thought as she washed her hands, it was both of them competing for mirror space in the small en suite bathroom, two young married people in a hurry to get to work. Once she was pregnant, though, she was quick to fall into the role of homemaker—almost immediately getting into the routine of prepping her husband's lunch, kissing him goodbye at the door and then starting into the vacuuming and laundry. Somewhere along the way, she'd got bored and launched Katt Basket, but she'd have to get back to work soon if she wasn't pregnant; her skills had a shelf life, and if she let them sit unused too long, she'd end up useless

"Hey, hey, hey, gotta rush, gotta a rush," Josh said, coming down the hall fast, pant legs swishing. She met him at the pass-through, leaning over next to his lunch bag, lips pouted for a kiss.

Josh came in for the kiss, paused and regarded her with her lips pooched out, and the momentary pause got her laughing, imagining what her face looked like to him. Josh took her lapels and brought her close. She re-formed the kissing shape, and they brought their mouths together.

"Mm-wah," she pronounced as their kiss came apart, but Josh still held the front of her robe. Their eyes connected and she saw he was troubled and for two terrible heartbeats she imagined someone from Tiffany's party had posted a rumor on Facebook . . . But Josh smiled, his cute mouth tucking to one side. The smile, reluctant and sheepish—boyish still even though he was reaching thirty—relaxed her, and a warm soothing feeling traveled up her back.

Very serious in tone now, he said, "Tonight I'll do better."

She had a feeling about his meaning but asked him to clarify, eyes narrowed and expression also serious.

That Josh smile went to one side again, then he said, "You know what I mean—I'll show you I can do better."

Now she put her hands on his lapels, straightened his tie and pretended to tighten the knot. She bit her lip to look sexy, saying, "I'm looking forward to it—see if you can keep off the bourbon at work today."

There was a sting displayed in his eyes and she regretted what she said—just trying to be funny and all. Josh rolled with it, going unusually sexual, saying in a husky voice: "Might want to have a nap today, rest up."

"Well, well, well," she whispered, surprised by his sexual forwardness. Their eyes remained connected for a long moment, both of them looking puzzled as they studied each other.

At last Josh said, "I'm going to be late."

"You better get going," she said, smoothing her hands on his lapels, the shine of her wedding ring catching her attention.

Josh pecked her lips again, snatched his lunch bag off the island counter, and headed for the hall. "Thanks for making lunch, Kimmy," he said, leaning on the closet doors so he could slip sock feet into leather shoes.

She came to stand and watch from the kitchen, warm coffee mug held in both hands at her chest. "Don't get too excited; celery, mustard, and mushrooms on a whole wheat pita."

"Mm-mm-mm," Josh hummed and looked up. "All my favorites."

"See you tonight," she said chuckling and then there was this awkward moment where Josh looked like he might come in and kiss her again, and she stood funny and flat-footed ready to receive him then he appeared to change his mind and gave her a lopsided smile, standing there like he didn't know what to do with his hands. It was like they were in high school, two nervous teenagers unsure of how the other felt about them.

"See ya," Josh said and slung his lunch bag over a shoulder, grabbed his keys and briefcase and opened their apartment door.

"Bye, Josh," she said, coming into the hall as he slipped out backward, smiling still and being weird.

It made her chuckle—it was clear he was on the

verge of chuckling, too, recognizing their strangeness —and she stood by the door for half a minute, making sure he wasn't going to return before she turned over the deadbolt.

There was another long quiet moment as she stood in the center of the living room considering the damage she'd done, the hurt she'd caused to a man who didn't deserve it. Josh was kind, he was caring, and his life centered around her. If he discovered what happened at the party, he would be devastated and she could never forgive herself. The urge to come clean was strong. If she was honest with Josh, she could escape the whirlwind of bad thoughts. She exhaled hugely, let it all out, waited till that exhaled air had cleared and then breathed again.

She walked to the windows and watched down at the parking lot as her husband crossed the macadam making his way to the Nissan. Back door opened, he loaded in his things then got in the driver's. The car started, and still she watched. Josh was innocent, unsuspecting. Maybe not that unsuspecting, though, asking all those questions last night about the nature of her interaction with Devlin Stone.

"Devlin Stone," she whispered now, then shivered, hearing his name out loud.

Maybe in time she would tell Josh. It might even be survivable. But that was selfish because that was considering their relationship. It was Josh's feelings that she wanted spared. It was noble in its own illicit way. She'd prefer to suffer in the knowledge of what she'd done than to have it delivered to Josh's ears. It wasn't an affair—what had happened between her and Devlin had nothing to do with feelings. Her love for Josh was unblemished and pure despite the awfulness of her actions. She could lie, say she was drunk too. But what was the point in trying to come clean in a muddy spray of lies?—she would be no better off. For now, she would keep this to herself and suffer in silence. If she was lucky—no, if Josh was lucky— everyone else could keep their mouths shut. If she could make it past this first week, she figured Josh might be okay. People forget, people have new things to gossip about. Just one week.

After breakfast, she cleaned the kitchen, swept, vacuumed and took a load of laundry down the hall and got it washing. Then she had a hot shower, got in a soft T-shirt and some old jeans that had worn till they felt like velvet, and got herself in the studio, and fired up a Chinese-dubbed episode 13 of The Heirs.

One basket today. One-a-day and she could keep on top of the orders, and the extra income was nice until it was time to go back to work for real. Or get pregnant, Kimmy.

Or get pregnant. You could do that too.

Her phone text-chimed as she unloaded supplies from the huge shelving unit Josh bought her at the Pickering Market, a perfectly usable purchase that left her wondering how on earth her husband would know her workflow. The thing came from an old public school, she imagined; a heavy duty set of wooden shelves that had seen some use, all the edges worn smooth, dinged and marked by nicks, spotted and striped by the occasional small graffito (AJ hearts DR) or marker smudge. Josh had taken it apart in Steve's garage and he and Steve loaded it into Steve's pickup truck one Saturday and the two of them hustled it up to her studio and re-assembled it while she was out grocery shopping.

With the wealthy students of Jeguk High living out love and drama in the background, a steaming cup of tea on the worktable, knuckles cracked, she was ready to get lost in a meditative 36 x 18 tight-octagon-weave triangle-rush basket for some lady's cat all the way in Oregon. She flipped over her phone. . . . Then wished she hadn't.

Underneath a text from Amy that had arrived while she was in the shower, she saw the name Devlin Stone. He'd sent her a message.

Devlin Stone: I think we need to talk

5
MONDAYS

The morning had been difficult at first, getting into work, and all that was on his mind was Kimmy. There was a sick and sinking feeling in his stomach, a heavy feeling he wished he could shake but was unable. The events of the weekend weighed on him, so did his performance last night. The revelation, too, that Kimmy was looking to conceive again and they hadn't discussed it at all. Of course he was ready, it was just sprung on him unexpectedly. Add to that the awkward exchange with his own wife this morning when he was leaving for work. What the hell was that about? He felt like he did back in high school and he wasn't dating her and he just had that god-awful crush feeling. Shit, that's that feeling in his stomach—that's exactly what it was like.

Steve was in the office already when he pulled in, parked next to his pickup truck, but he didn't get a chance to talk until their break at 10:15. So over a croissant, he ambled around the subject of the weird weekend he'd had. Steve brought it up first, asking him how his reunion went. Josh started the story casually, saying how he and Kimmy had fun back at Dalton, how weird it was seeing the old school, how everything seemed so much smaller than it did when he was younger; the place had little of the dread he'd attributed to it when he attended. The dinner had been fine. It was weird seeing all those familiar faces changed by time and maturity. Steve asked how the party at the lake was. Steve didn't attend Dalton, didn't grow up in Kingston at all, but over their time at A.J. Swanson Market Research, they'd become quite good friends. He'd told him how weird it was going to Tiffany's cottage because she was the rich girl in their high school, the pretty one, and Steve could commiserate because hell, every high school had one of those girls in one form or the other. So Josh told him the truth, said how it was fun. Surprisingly fun. And it had been at first—probably why he felt loosened up enough to drink too much. While he'd been friendly with Tiffany in school (or at least not enemies) there was a certain trepidation dealing with her kind, so when he got there and most of that angst from high school had dissipated, there was a noticeable lightening of spirit. Plus, Amy was there, and he hadn't seen her in so long, and Karina too, who was a good friend. Tiffany had left the invitation to her party open to anyone, not a select few. So there were plenty of people he knew there who also weren't in with Tiff's crowd. But this is where the story got difficult—but it was also the part of the story he was most intrigued by, and looking for a good soundboard to bounce with for feedback.

Only how was he going to relate the part where Devlin had come into his tent and showed him his erection? That was way too weird, wasn't it? What the hell would Steve think of that? And how would he relate what it was that Devlin had said: that Josh had proposed he surrender his wife to the more alpha male, and that Devlin was there to say it was done? Want proof?—smell your wife's pussy on my huge dick. Yeah, that would not be said.

THE CAFETERIA WHERE EVERYONE TOOK THEIR break at Swanson was a cavernous space that could probably seat a hundred people. But for now, the 10:15 to 10:30 break time, there were only maybe forty workers, all in shirts and ties, skirts and slacks, gathered in small clutches at the tables. Josh and Steve had a spot by the towering windows looking over the parking lot, shielded from the sun this time of day by honey locusts that rimmed the walkways outside the building.

Josh delayed for time, wedging the blade of a stainless knife to pry up the top layer of the croissant, drizzled in zigzags with white and brown chocolate stripes. He took the buttery wafer, put it in his mouth.

Steve could sense something was up, putting his bagel back down on the plate and looking at him. "So then what happened?"

Josh said, "These two guys from the lacrosse team, this guy Winston, this other guy whose last name was Zephyr—everybody calls him Zeph—come out to where we're sitting with bottles of bourbon."

"Oh, Jesus," Steve said, then laughed.

"Oh, Jesus is right. So I'm at a table with Kimmy, those two guys from lacrosse, Kimmy's friend Amy from England, this other girl Stephanie . . . I'm in a good mood..."

"I can see where this is going."

"Right," Josh said, raising his eyebrows, looking at his croissant. "So we're doing shots of bourbon—"

"My stomach's queasy already."

"I *like* bourbon. And this was good bourbon. We weren't doing shots, it was just going into plastic cups and being sipped . . . but I *kept* drinking . . . It was *really* good bourbon."

"What did you do?" Steve said in a tone that suggested the story would end somewhere embarrassing.

"Well . . . I drank too much."

"Did Kimmy drink?"

"You know Kimmy doesn't drink."

"No, no," Steve said and was smiling—the smile making Josh feel all right for a moment or two, forgetting that there were elements of the story too terrible to relate.

He said, "Anyway, I drank too much. Kimmy had to help me into our tent. I don't know what happened after that."

"That's it? I thought you were going to tell me you went streaking or something."

"No, that wasn't me. A couple guys went skinny-dipping when I was passed out."

"So you didn't do anything?"

"No, I just drank too much. End of story. But here's the thing," he said now, tongue working around his mouth as he shifted his seat closer to the table. He leaned over, spoke quieter even though there was no one else nearby, and everyone at the other tables engaged in their own stories about their weekend adventures, an incessant murmuring chatter throughout the concrete and glass cavern. "When I wake up, there's like this big kerfuffle when I go into the house."

Steve wiped his mouth with a napkin. "What's a kerfuffle?"

"I go into the cottage, and it's like Kimmy has been in a fight."

"Oh, shit."

"Right? Like she's not even talking to me, but all her girlfriends are around her, and all like rubbing her arms, telling her it's okay."

"Who'd she fight with?"

"It wasn't a girl. It was a guy."

"Oh, yeah?"

"This guy she hated back in high school—we all

hated back in high school. This guy Devlin Stone. His dad owns like this import-export business in Kingston, real hot shot. Super rich."

"What'd she fight about?"

"She won't really tell me."

"That's weird."

"At the party I'm asking what's up, and everybody's saying hey just chill out, let Kimmy deal with it, so I do. But I'm like seriously hung the fuck over, man, like seeing double, on the verge of puking, so it's totally easy for me to lay back and let it all play out."

"So what happened?"

"Kimmy deals with it. That guy Devlin is there, and she goes over and they're talking it out. I'm standing by trying not to throw up, trying to maintain my dignity. I keep expecting all the pieces to fall into place, you know?"

"What'd she say happened?"

"That's just the thing. She didn't say what it was."

"She didn't tell you what they fought about?" Steve showed a look of puzzlement—almost disbelief, like he was taking Kimmy's side already, good old Josh blowing this out of proportion and making it a bigger deal than it was.

"Yeah, I know that's not like Kimmy," he said, "but she was still riled up. We left the party, like right away, she's saying she's gotta get out of there, we get in the car and I'm right out, sleeping instantly. I go home, I sleep some more, wake up and I feel better."

"And you asked what happened?"

"I did," he said, shrugged and poked the croissant.

Steve said, "She didn't tell you what happened?"

"She said she argued with him."

"About what?"

"Politics."

"Yeah, so they don't see eye-to-eye. This some rich-kid white guy?—I can already see where this is going."

"I know," he said, shaking his head, unsure of where to take the story next.

Steve said, "Josh, man, she told you what it was. She said they fought about politics."

"I don't know about what though," he said, "because she doesn't want to talk about it."

"Maybe she's embarrassed."

"I can get that. But of all the people in the world she could talk to, aren't I one of them? Couldn't she tell me why she's upset?"

"I suppose, but I don't think it's a big deal—"

"She said they *physically* fought, too, that she tried to hit him, and he grabbed her arms."

Steve frowned. "Oh . . . oh, shit."

"See? Holy shit, right?"

"That doesn't sound like Kimmy."

"Thank God," Josh said, laughing now and looking up at the high ceiling. "Thank God, you see it."

"Yeah, but so?"

"But so? . . . She gets in a fight with some guy and she won't tell me what it's about?"

"Josh, what are you saying?" Steve held up his hands like the answer was obvious, but he couldn't believe the implication.

"What?"

Steve said, "She's embarrassed. . . . That's not like Kimmy at all. Getting in a fist fight with somebody? When has she ever been in a fight? When's she ever even raised her voice?" Steve took a moment to laugh. "Look, she's embarrassed. She doesn't want to talk about it. You could be a good guy and leave her alone."

"I did leave her alone."

"Maybe she'll tell you sometime. It's Monday. She's probably still stinging over it, whatever it was."

"You're probably right." He poked at his croissant again, put his cheek in his palm.

"Fuck," Steve said, laughing now, lighter. "The way you were dancing around it there, I thought you were trying to say something . . . *happened*."

"Something happened?"

"Between the two of them."

Now he frowned. "Do you think that could have happened?"

"No way. That was my point. I was about to slap you in the noggin. If that's what you think, you're out of your mind. . . . Kimmy's not like that. She's just embarrassed."

"I hope that's it."

"That's totally it. Or, shit, maybe *you* embarrassed her."

His stomach tightened at the thought. "You think I could've?"

"She said you just passed out?"

"She did."

Steve looked away, thought a moment. "Maybe that's part of it. I don't know." When Steve looked back at him, he was smirking.

Josh laughed, relieved Steve'd meant it as a joke. "Why would you even say that?"

Steve laughed too, said, "Because sometimes I can't imagine what she's even doing with you."

Josh arrived home at his usual time, 5:45. Parked, elevator up, trudging to the apartment door, bushed, a terrible cramp running from both sides of his neck down his shoulders. Hangover residue. But he'd made it through the shift at work, and tomorrow was another day.

When he went in the apartment, it was dark.

"Kimmy?"

There was no smell of cooking, and for a moment he thought maybe she was out.

But Kimmy answered then, saying, "Hi, Josh," her voice coming from the kitchen. He slipped off his shoes, joined her by the fridge, Kimmy putting her phone down. Hand on her waist, they kissed. She asked him how his day went.

"Well, I made it through."

She asked him how he was feeling and put her

hands on his cheeks, the coolness of her hands making him feel feverish. "I feel fine. My back's a little sore, but I had no headaches or nausea . . ."

"That's good. You ready for dinner?"

He asked her what she was making, showing a look of puzzlement glancing around the kitchen that had obviously been cleaned and not seen any duty since.

"Dinner's in twenty minutes."

Still puzzled, he asked what they were having.

"Your favorite."

Now it was coming clearer. "Wait a second . . . Bifanas?"

"I called our order soon as I saw you pull into the parking lot."

"God, Kimmy, that's great," he said. "I'm starving. The bitoque?"

"With fries," she said, rubbing his arm.

Bifanas was a Portuguese place, the bitoque his favorite, a steak and egg dish served with rice and olives, and fries if you wanted. Kimmy asked him if he'd like a Coke now.

He looked down at what he was wearing. "I just walked in the door."

"Go get changed," she said.

When he gave her a funny face showing her actions were strange, she laughed, came and kissed his cheek. "I missed you today."

"I missed you too," he said.

"You want to play some Red Dead Redemption?"

"You going to go to the gym?"

She shook her head no.

He walked down the hall, glancing back to see Kimmy heading into the family room. It was quite the welcome. Not completely unusual, but there was still something bothering him. At her studio, he stopped; the lights were off, but he poked his head in. On the worktable there was an array of rush grass partially woven, forming the base of the basket, the ends of the grass spread around the base like a child's drawing of the sun. He went into the bedroom and changed, putting on sweatpants, shorts, and a T-shirt, coming back out to the family room. Kimmy was on the couch, the Xbox turned on, a glass of Coke poured and resting on the coffee table.

He said, "Boy, you're really going all out tonight."

She took the compliment, laughing.

"I like it," he said. "I should get drunk and embarrass you more often."

"Don't you dare," she said and narrowed her eyes at him slyly. With her back against the couch's arm, she lay stretched out wearing soft cotton pants, her legs casually crossed over, feet bare.

He pinched her toe, and she smiled. "Sorry about the party."

Kimmy raised her eyebrows and made an expression like it was all in the past anyway, saying, "I told you I didn't want to talk about it."

He offered up: "If I did something really stupid, if I did something that really embarrassed you, you don't have to spare my feelings. I want to know the truth."

"You didn't do anything except drink too much and pass out, Josh."

"You certain?"

She pointed to the floor at her side, indicating for him to take his spot where he liked to sit with his back on the couch and play video games. And her request was so inviting and warm, he was quick to surrender all his doubt and hurt, and threw himself happily at her side. He played a few minutes of Red Dead Redemption before the apartment buzzer went off, the Door Dash driver in the lobby. "I'll get it," she said, "you keep playing."

He did, Kimmy paying the guy, taking the bags into the kitchen and preparing plates for each of them then bringing them out to the coffee table. Game paused for the moment, they watched TV while they ate.

After dinner, when Kimmy took the dishes to the kitchen to clean, leaving him to play Xbox, he got a text from Devlin Stone.

6

REMOTE CONTROL

The words from his bully written out on his phone's screen chilled him. All the fear he'd experienced this weekend came rushing back to him in all its former glory. Part of him, thirty-six hours removed, had come to believe that maybe Devlin in the tent had been a dream after all, that the horror wrapping itself around him was all fabricated in his own mind, woven from blades of past trauma like one of Kimmy's baskets.

A simple friendly phrase, yet one heavy with the threat of what would come next.

how's it going?

The query wasn't preceded by Devlin Stone's name, but by a phone number Josh didn't recognize. Yet he knew it wasn't spam or a mistake, he *knew* it was Devlin. He stared at the words a long time, opened his phone and his message app, texted a reply.

> Josh: leave me alone

A reply came in a few seconds.

> don't be sore

He texted again:

> Josh: leave me alone

On the TV screen his cowboy sat atop a chestnut mare, a mountain vista spread out before them. He set the controller down and rubbed his fingers against his clammy palms.

Another text:

> Kimmy say I came by to talk to her today?

He grunted, disbelieving this was his reality again after he'd thought they'd moved on. His face had tightened, his brow lowered, but his shoulders slumped like they were too heavy.

> Josh: fuck off

> she didn't? bad girl that Kimmy

Josh: I don't believe you

why not?

Now he looked over his shoulder and could see his wife in the kitchen, through the pass-thru, moving around with her back to him, her black hair tied back in a tail.

Josh: go fuck with someone else

Josh just go and ask her

I didn't fuck her if that's what you're thinking

His fingers tingled like he'd been sitting on them, and he felt detached from his body, watching himself from above sitting on the couch gawking at his phone, Xbox controller and fizzing Coke on the table at his knees. There was a profound feeling of unreality.

Josh: that's good

feel better?

Josh: no go away

I mean she begged me to fuck her and I had her pants down

There was a clinking and clattering in the kitchen, Kimmy loading the dishwasher. He regarded her over his shoulder again, and the sight of her feminine form, its innocent grace, had him angry that Devlin would fabricate something so horrible. The image of Kimmy begging Devlin Stone to fuck her couldn't even be formed. Fantasy was one thing, but bringing the image closer to realism was impossible.

He turned back, admired the mountain view beyond his cowboy's horse.

Josh: you are so full of shit

Am I?

The anger tightening his neck and jaw was welcome and comforting in its way. He chuckled a confrontational sound, texted.

Josh: Big successful guy like you has nothing better to do on a Monday night than fuck around with some guy from high school? Pretty sad man

ha ha, Josh, you got me. I'm eating dinner at Harbour 60 right now so bored I gotta text my old pal Josh and make up a story how I fingered his wife today

Now he was practically growling, a low animal

sound in his throat. he was too grown up to be a bully's victim now.

> Josh: you grew up to be a real piece of shit

I left you something

> Josh: oh okay

Oh okay. He liked the sound of it. He smiled, betting to himself Devlin hadn't expected Josh to be so aloof this time around. But he wasn't blitzed with bourbon, roused from a painful sleep. Now he was comfortable at home, on his own couch, recovered, well-fed and tended by the woman he loved. A woman who would never sleep with Devlin Stone.

So this would be where a bully like Devlin Stone was going to say something perverse and mean and belittling, and he could see it in his mind before it was even written: *Left you my sloppy seconds . . .* Practically followed by imagined wheezy teenage laughter. Only he and Devlin were removed from school a long time now—*so fuck off, Devlin, you're powerless over adults.*

But it wasn't what Devlin returned.

Nice apartment you have

He stared at the statement a long time. It got him. Well played, Devlin.

Josh: thanks

small, plain, there's a picture of
Taiwan in the eighties b&w on the
wall facing you as you come in the
door. brown leather couches in the
family room, you have a wedding
photo on the table against the wall...

There wasn't much to say, so he just read, winding
his neck around as he did, that helpful anger
fumbling, getting into the backseat now so worry
could get up and take the wheel.

nothing to say now? I told you I left
you something. Go in the front hall,
the table where there's the flowers
and the dish with coins and keys,
open the top drawer for me

Josh: Why?

I left something for you

Josh: it's not there

you didn't check then

Josh: I don't have to

coward

When he rose from the couch, his legs were

shaky. He stared a moment at the cowboy on screen waiting for his input, waiting to be led into great and wonderful adventures. Instead, he was a player on someone else's screen, his high school bully's, a piece in another man's fantasy adventure.

In the kitchen, Kimmy still puttered, content and oblivious. It angered him she would be brought in on this malicious enterprise, an innocent NPC—it was the challenge to her honor that got his heart pounding again. How dare Devlin say these terrible things about her? But he was stuck now, somewhere between the anger and the submission, his feet moving across the apartment floor, taking him to the front hall where he would confirm what Devlin was saying wasn't true.

The awful journey to his front hall was his bully's joy, he was sure, sitting gleefully on the other end of this text exchange picturing dumb Josh shitting his pants in Ajax. He'd come to find the drawer empty and Devlin would then say Kimmy must have found it first and got rid of it. String this game along further, drag gullible Josh out into deeper waters.

Only, when he made it to the front hall unspotted by Kimmy, he opened the drawer of the table with the flowers and the dish of keys and coins and found Devlin was right. There on the top layer of junk, right at the far side, a crisp linen business card lay face up and staring like it had been expecting him. *What took you so long, Mr. Waters* it was saying. The chills and the tingles returned to him, that sinking feeling in his stomach pushing down hard on his bladder. The card read: Stone Custom Brokerage LLC, then in bolder font, the cardholder's name, Devlin Stone, and, underneath in italics, Vice-President.

He never lifted the card from where it sat, left it there, and quietly closed the drawer again. Kimmy still cleaned, still oblivious to the tragedy in the front hall, scooting around the kitchen in her slippers.

When he looked down, there was another message waiting for him on his phone.

> Kimmy's way too much woman
> for you

The sinking feeling deepened, the anger liquifying and pooling around his feet.

> Josh: U came here today

> I did. Believe me now?

> Josh: Why?

> I told you you asked me to fuck
> Kimmy

> Josh: I never asked that

> You sure did

Josh: I don't want that

You told me you did

Josh: Now I'm telling you I don't

He stared at the screen, waiting for the response. It came.

Too late

He grumbled a pained sound, thumbs flying.

Josh: Don't text me again don't ever come by my apartment again and don't talk to Kimmy

Too late for all that Josh Kimmy and I have something good going

Josh: I'm telling you to stop

You know you want it, now I want it. And Kimmy wants it too

Josh: No she doesn't.

enjoy it man you asked for it you're getting it

ciao

. . .

THERE WAS NO WAY IT COULD BE TRUE.

It had to be a ruse, but he was standing there in the front hall with all the demonstrated proof someone would need. And yet there was a surprising emptiness inside him. It was like the horror was currently buoyed on the vestiges of his disbelief.

He moved to the kitchen doorway, could see Kimmy rinsing a plate, the dishwasher open, placing it on the bottom rack. She was done now, drying her hands.

Something occurred to him. Something that had registered in his mind, but sat dormant until now. He approached her, took the towel from her hands, her smiling and watching him suspiciously. He snapped away the wet towel, then folded it and tossed it onto the counter. She asked him what was up.

He took her hands, kissed her knuckles. "Thank you for dinner."

"I slaved away all afternoon," she said, averting her eyes.

Now he held both her hands between them, thumbing her knuckles, caressing her wedding ring. He said, "Did your nails today, eh?"

Sure enough, the thing that had registered: Kimmy had changed her nail color. There'd been a clear coat over a base of dusty rose for the high school reunion. Hadn't changed that yesterday, but now he could see she'd done them in black.

She took her hands away from his, looked at her nails. "Oh yeah, I did."

"Black, huh?"

"I was bored," she said.

"Bored?"

She shrugged, and her lack of forthcoming irked him. He said, "You weren't busy today? Did you get a basket and a half done?"

"No," she said, eyes straying away again.

"You didn't?" There was an unfinished basket on her worktable.

She said, "Just a half a basket."

"Did you go out?"

"No . . . My hands were sore," she said now, then shook one of them out as if it was still smarting. She made a fist, then wouldn't look his way again.

"Are your hands sore?"

"Yeah, a little . . ." Then: "I just didn't feel like it today. I started watching The Heirs, I lost track of time. Next thing I know, I'm making tea, I got my feet up . . . I did my fingernails."

"While you watched Netflix?"

"Yes," she said, unsmiling, then adding, "My toes, too," looking down at her feet though she wore slippers in the house.

He said, "Are you okay?"

"Yeah," she said, posture slumping. "I'm okay . . ." She leaned on the counter and crossed her arms.

"Anybody come by today?"

Though she made no reaction at all, somehow

that was a weird indication by itself. Kimmy stone-faced him. Gave him her lawyer face. When she wanted to, she could keep you out—it was part of what she practiced, never letting your opponent know what you've got. She said, "No . . . why?"

He shrugged, looked away. "Just wondering."

There was a beat of quiet, then: "What does that mean?"

"I don't know, like Amy or something. Maybe you guys went out . . ."

"I said I didn't go out."

"Well, it's just . . ."

She stared at him a long while with her lips parted, an expression somewhere between concern and anger. She said finally: "Why would you ask me that?"

"I said I don't know. It's weird coming home to you like this."

"Like what?—I ordered your favorite dinner, Josh. You played video games, we ate together. What's wrong with that?"

"There's *nothing* wrong with that, Kimmy," he said and put up his hands. "Look," he said, backing away, not wanting to be a part of this conversation at all anymore. "You're being weird, so I'm asking you questions."

"Your questions are weird, Josh, like you sound like you're accusing me of something."

"You're acting like you're guilty. I'm asking ques-tions. I'm not chasing you, I'm following you."

Her eyes darted over his, she softened then, raised her eyebrows. "Sorry," she said, and now he was the guilty one.

He went to her, saying, "It's okay . . . I don't mean to bug you. It's just..."

"What—because I won't tell you about..." She left the sentence unfinished. *The argument at the party.*

"Yeah, I don't know."

"It's nothing, Josh. Don't make it into something."

"You're making into something by being so tightlipped."

She studied him again, eyes going over his, weighing and measuring.

He said, "What are you thinking?"

"Nothing," she said softly.

"All right," he said, backing away again. I'm going to be in my office."

IN HIS OFFICE, JOSH FOUND HIMSELF OBSESSED WITH disproving Devlin's texted taunts, searching Facebook now for proof. It was a convenient escape from dwelling on the almost-confrontation with Kimmy. It would be a mistake to let Devlin get in his head, infect his marriage. Not without confirmation.

Disbelief—wondrous and welcome disbelief—had begun to leak again into his mind. You couldn't trust Devlin. What Devlin accused Kimmy of was ridiculous. Why would he take for granted the words texted to him from a malicious man who'd made his youth precarious? It was a magic trick, was all. Now he just had to figure the trick, learn the sleight of hand.

So now he was operating on the presumption that Devlin's description of his apartment, while accurate, was a distraction. It was meant to bolster his belief in stage two of Devlin's trick: the business card.

Devlin's description of his apartment sounded contrived when Josh replayed it in his head, and now he was checking his and Kimmy's Facebook photos for instances Devlin could have gleaned; shots from Josh and Kimmy's married life that showed the inside of their apartment. While he scoured, proof still eluded him; there were no definitive images that showed the front hall, though there were other pictures of the apartment that showed the family room and the brown leather couches. The description still stuck funny in his mind-ear: superficial, paint-by-numbers, as though Devlin was never in the apartment but had seen a photo or had been given a second-hand description.

He had to consider that Devlin may not be alone in this particular campaign of domination. The act of humiliation was best with an audience, and back at high school Devlin always had compatriots's faces leering nearby to join in on the vicious hilarity.

Here was the thing about the business card: If Devlin wanted to drop a big whammy and he was so fucking smart he would have left a note, maybe a message, something with his name . . . Just a business card? Come on, that was low grade for a bully like Devlin Stone—what, he was going to pass up the opportunity to write a note like *Kimmy's pussy is so tight*, right on the card? Some real low blow knife-stab.

What if it wasn't Devlin at all he'd been texting with? Like Steve was fucking with him after their talk today. Only how would Steve get Devlin Stone's business card? *Shit, what's wrong with you, Josh?* It might not even *be* Stone's business card. Anybody could do a business card up on a computer and print it out. Steve, maybe, arranging some prank with Kimmy even. It was far-fetched, but so was Devlin coming by here today and fingering Kimmy. Shit, Steve wouldn't have the guts to text those dirty things on the messages about Kimmy. Even as a joke, he could never type out that he'd fingered Kimmy—it would creep him out.

Kimmy snuck up on him while he was lost in a Facebook wormhole, his monitor faced away from the door, so he could see her in the hall, on her way to the bedroom. She stopped in the doorway, resting a hand, then her forehead on the frame.

"Hey," he said.

"I'm going to go to bed," she said.

"You are?"

She nodded, head still on the frame, bending one knee so she could plant her toes on the floor and wag her calf side to side.

"It's not even nine."

She shrugged, said, "Good night, baby," slunk away from the frame and lingered a second before resuming her path down the hall. But she came back.

His hand rolled the mouse around in a circle, his cursor going in concentric lines on the monitor, peering over top to see what she would say. Kimmy slunk against the frame again and showed an uncomfortable aura of guilt. It showed in the bowing of her eyebrows, the slump of her shoulders. Kimmy didn't know Devlin had sent him taunts over messaging, but she did know her husband had questioned her in a way he'd never done before. If she were innocent, she would be mad, perplexed; if she were guilty, what then?

Kimmy said, "Can you come to bed with me?"

And the sight of her this way made him the guilty one, thinking of her the way he'd been thinking, allowing another man to control him, manipulate him, ruin what he had with his Kimmy. Below the wide cuff of her cotton capris, her ankles were slender; the string straps of her feathery tank top drew thin lines on her graceful shoulders; her black hair hung shaggy around her angular but sweet and innocent face, her black eyes watching him, bright and wet.

If she'd had sex with Devlin today, would she really want you in the bed right now? Would she want more sex? Wouldn't she be worn out?

Come on, the whole thing's ludicrous . . . Plus, searching Facebook was futile; a picture of their apartment could be on someone else's page, not his or Kimmy's. They'd had parties here before, so maybe someone posted a pic and Devlin'd seen it.

He said, "I'm coming."

He followed her down the hall to their bedroom, Kimmy closing the door behind them and leaving the lights off. He stood in the quiet, turned, felt her body up against his. Kimmy kissed his neck and put her arms around his waist. He said, "I'm sorry for before."

She said nothing, continued kissing his neck, her nails drawing circles on his lower back now. She didn't want to talk, didn't bring him in here for conversation, so he better smarten up. And, before he knew it, her hand was groping his junk over his sweatpants, right hand squeezing and kneading his penis and testicles over the cotton while her mouth sought his. He kissed her. She whispered, "I had a nap today . . ."

"That's good."

"You told me to nap, so I'd be rested."

"So you rested?" *Wow, some dirty talker, Josh.*

"Are you going to fuck me, baby?"

Hearing his wife say something so harsh was unexpected, and he flinched at her dirty language. He whispered, "Yeah."

"What are you going to do to me?"

"Make love to you."

"Yeah? . . . How?" Now she ran her thigh up his

knee, getting a foot right off the floor. She squeezed his balls, lifted them up, taking his sweatpants along and flossing him a wedgie. Kimmy was horned up in a way he couldn't remember before. Maybe back in early college, or, shoot, in high school when they first started doing it and jumped at any chance, going from 0 to 60 in seconds, teenage hormones in hyperdrive. But in their adult life, his Kimmy wasn't ever so forward. It was intimidating.

"I don't know…"

"Tell me, Josh, tell me what you're going to do to me."

Her hand kneaded his genitals more eagerly, and she went on her toes so she could hook an arm around his neck and kiss his mouth. He put his hands on her finally, and they moved like they were timid, touching her back, caressing, being kind and polite. Fuck, just like in high school, and it was the first time they were together.

And now it was in his head. *Kimmy's way too much woman for you.* Was it true? As she matured, Kimmy was undeniably acquiring a powerful sexiness. The shaggy bangs, the full raven head of hair framing her intelligent face. The slim smile lines around her perfect pouting mouth. Those sexy brown eyes in their narrow almond shapes. Could she do better? You don't deserve Kimmy—that's what Devlin was saying. And if another man came for her and he had to compete, what really was it he could offer a woman like Kimmy? Their legacy? Even Steve saying today he couldn't imagine what Kimmy saw in him. Just joking around—he was sure of it—but now with everything else going on, it provoked amazing insecurity. It was just like back in high school, when they first started going out together. He didn't know if it was a real thing or not. He crushed on Kimmy Chang so hard, and when she agreed to go out, he feared the whole night she thought it was just as friends. And he was too worried to make a move, worried he would offend her. But she was his wife now. They'd got past all the act, and so his hands grew bolder, squeezing at her ribs, moving down to cup her ass cheeks. Kimmy complied right away, sighing into his mouth and parting her legs wider. He slipped a hand down the back of her cotton pants, right underneath her panties. He found his wife warm and wet already, his two middle fingers sliding along her slick groove, already well-oiled and hungry.

"Oh, Josh," she murmured, and he probed them inside. She raised her knee higher, hooked the inside of her thigh on his hipbone, desperate for him to penetrate her. He slid his fingers deeper, and she whispered, "Tell me what you're going to do to me."

"I don't know, Kimmy..."

"You had all day. . . . What did you fantasize?"

It was true—the weird thing was, he hadn't really thought about it. He'd warned her this morning to be prepared, and selfish Josh only thought about himself all day. . . . What did his wife do at the party? What was the fight about? Was it something I did? Was it something I said? Did I embarrass her? Me, me, me . . . But Kimmy wanted him. And wanted him now.

But his mind was poisoned.

She whispered, "Tell me something dirty. . . . Tell me something you want to do to me."

He froze, his mouth open, words eager to come out but frightened, hiding like timid voles in their tunnel. What would anything he said come out like? And the most frightening thing: he wasn't even really hard yet. She'd fondled him, squeezed him, kissed his neck, was eager and vocal—but now her arms were around him, scratching and caressing, and he could feel only a meager arousal in his underwear. Another replay of last night—*oh no...*

"Tell me, Josh, tell me something dirty."

"I don't know, Kimmy. . . . Let's move to the bed."

Kimmy made a disappointed sound and let him go. He couldn't see her in the dark, but now was imagining her impatient, disappointed. It sunk him. His erection completely dwindled, he put his hands out to find her. She was gone. He could hear her getting on the bed now, and he was quick to join her, wanting to show her it wasn't over.

ONLY HE DIDN'T FIND HER LAYING IN BED. THE silhouette of his wife loomed on his right-hand side, Kimmy sitting on the edge of the bed. The act of sitting disheartened him. Not laying in bed looking for a second attempt at lovemaking, but sitting. . . .

And sitting was the position where you *talked* rather than made love.

He scooted to join her, both of them looking out the bedroom windows at the starlight sky. She asked him what was wrong.

"Nothing's wrong, Kimmy, I swear nothing's wrong."

"Don't you want to...?" She looked his way, and he could see her concerned face bathed by the outdoor light.

"Of course I do. How could I not want to? . . . It's not that at all. I just felt . . . I don't know..."

"Is it me?"

"No. It's a lot of pressure. I don't..."

"I'm putting pressure on you?"

"I'm sorry."

She hung her head, said, "I'm sorry too. I mean, Josh, it's . . . it's just sex. Don't you want to fuck me?"

"It's a lot," he said, wishing he'd just grow up and lay her back and make love to her the way he wanted —shit, the way *she* wanted. But his arousal had evaporated, so he was useless right now, anyway. So he said, "It's a lot, telling me to tell you what I'm going to do."

"I'm sorry, Josh. Can we start over?"

And now he felt guilty as well as limp. He said, "No, don't be sorry, it's not your fault at all. I told you I was going to make things right tonight, but I don't know . . . When we came in here, and you started saying those things."

"I thought you might like that."

"I do," he said—and, what the fuck, of course he did. . . . Why would he be challenged by her dirty talk? It was all because of Devlin Stone, this other guy getting in his head. All of it lies, all of it meant to hurt Josh remotely. That smug fuck sitting in a steakhouse manipulating loser Josh all the way in Ajax. Now the way he pictured it, it was Devlin and all those cronies from high school, guys from all the sports teams, them grown up now wearing suits and laughing at what cool-guy Devlin was doing to this nerd. How could he let someone get in his head like that? It was impossible to think what Devlin said was true.

Now he softened, looking at his wife's face, and she could see the change in him. They both smiled at each other, honest smiles, and then their mouths came together and they kissed. He played with her ear lobe, her hair, caressed her neck. She put her tongue in his mouth; soon her hand was back in his lap. It went to his knee, came up the inside of his thigh, began to squeeze and knead his manhood again. The fact he wasn't hard began to play at his weaknesses. Boy, imagine if Kimmy *had* been with Devlin today. What a difference. . . . Her husband with a smaller penis that didn't even work right. Devlin's text had said he fingered Kimmy, got her pants down. Now while he kissed her, the image came to him unbidden of his wife here in this bedroom, maybe up against the wall, right up against the apartment window where maybe the neighbors could see, submitting to this tall rich handsome fucking asshole. He could picture Devlin with his hands down her pants, Kimmy with her mouth hanging open, her eyes locked onto Devlin's eyes, Devlin's hand jacking inside her pants, slick wet sounds filling his room. His cheating wife.

Kimmy made an appreciative *cat*like sound—he realized he'd achieved full throbbing hardness, and she appreciated his earnest renewal. He had to strike while the iron was hot, leaning toward her now, Kimmy going to her back, him getting over top of her. She pushed his pants down and stroked his erection while they kissed.

His mind was stuck still, swirling around the idea of his wife at home while he was at work. A visitor comes by, a guy they all hate, but nobody would deny his appeal. It was the man that was objectionable, the package itself screamed success. And the fact that Kimmy, who'd never been charmed by men like that, would let Devlin put his hand in her pants had his cock aching to be inside her.

They shimmied higher onto the bed, Kimmy pushing her pants down. And he couldn't even wait for her top to come off, already shoving a knee between her legs, spreading them wider, Kimmy raising her knees and him getting between her legs. He thumbed his erection downward, found her opening easily, and slipped inside her. That thrilling entry into her body was poisoned by the notion of how she would be dominated by a man with Devlin's manhood. How would Kimmy react with Devlin? Now he could picture Kimmy like those overacting girls he watched in porn. Mewling little cats squirming all over the bed, saying crazy shit for muscular jerk-off guys with big dicks. Pictured his beloved smart and capable woman behaving that way. Her legs open, eager for another man...

He stabbed and stabbed, the bed creaking, Kimmy making soft, barely audible gasps in reaction to his thrusts. "Fuck, mm, fuck," he grunted, trying to shake away the thought of Kimmy with Devlin, but the fear that without it he would lose his arousal, coaxing him to ride it out just a little longer.

He could picture Kimmy sinking to her knees, doing down Devlin's zipper, then that thing Josh had seen in the tent beginning to protrude through the opening, inch after glorious inch, Kimmy's eyes widening as the hugest manhood imaginable was presented to her—Kimmy worshiping it, studying it, using her fingertips to caress it's hard ridged totem shapes. Then her mouth kissing it, her tongue caressing, sucking...

"Shit, oh shit..."

"Oh, Josh," Kimmy squeaked, and she hugged him tighter, one step ahead of him, knowing he was going to come before he even realized.

He spurted slippery lubrication inside her while conjuring terrible, horrible, frightening images of his wife with a man he hated—a man she hated—and the phantasmagoric movie in his mind's eye so powerful it triggered his system into powerful orgasm. He dug his elbows into the mattress over her shoulders, hunched his body, stabbed himself deep (aware at the moment of his orgasm she was taking everything he had right now, and how Devlin had a lot more) . . . He let that badness swirl like a dust devil ripping through the warehouse behind his eyes while throbbing waves of pleasure undulated through his body. His cock flexed and pulsed inside his wife, launching off a complete, copious, and powerful load inside her, Kimmy cooing and writhing, making light feathery circles on his back knowing her husband was ejaculating.

Shame rose, a sickly wool feeling up his back, his eyes widening, looking at her, seeing her beautiful hair spread out on the sheets they'd picked out together at the Jysk in Whitby. The terrible things he'd thought of her while encouraging his hardness and orgasm. . . . That man putting those images in his head.

Screw you, Devlin, because your little trick backfired.

Only, while he'd been successful, his pleasure achieved, it didn't exactly run the sexual gauntlet for Kimmy. She lay there and let her husband thrust into her for a couple minutes—was she supposed to be grateful that he could come? Wow, how great for Kimmy.

Now the happiness faded, and he was already

remorseful. "Sorry," he whispered, the endurance of his lovemaking an obvious failure.

"I'm glad you came," she said.

"I can go again."

"I got what I wanted," she said.

"Can we try again?"

She nodded, but her eyes were closed. He raised above her on straightened arms, his wife laying there with her top still on, her hair fanned around her angel face. He kissed her chin, and she patted his cheek.

The way her face was closed off left him with the idea she was concentrating on the seed he'd planted inside her body. That *should* make him happy, but still all he could think about was his disappointment. A man like Devlin would've ended the session much differently. He could picture Kimmy left sweating, a devastated mess after a long pounding session with Devlin. That's what girls said in high school. Had Kimmy ever heard that? Probably. So if she knew that, then she knew that what Josh'd just done wasn't good enough.

The earlier fears chased after him again: *You're not good enough for Kimmy*.

So much venom coursing through his system, he eased himself out from inside her, stood at the side of the bed. His pants were around his ankles, and he stooped to pick them up, kissed Kimmy's knee, but she didn't notice, raising her legs now, getting herself straighter on the bed and curling up on her back with her thighs hugged to her chest.

He backed away from her, saying, "I'm just gonna be a minute," and went to the bathroom.

* * *

THE WORRY'D BEEN JOSH HAD SEEN SOMETHING ON Facebook. Why else would he come at her like that, insinuating that she wasn't forthcoming about her activities today? Josh was never that way, had never questioned her or treated her like a liar. It'd made her think the rumors had started, people were talking, and soon everyone would know what Kimmy and Devlin had got up to at the party. They'd never understand. And the hurt to Josh was unconscionable.

Only now it was worse than yesterday.

With her toes spread on the bathroom floor, seated on the toilet, Josh's seed spilling from her, she twirled fingers through her folds, pulling back on her hood and mushing down on her clit, chasing down something she wanted very bad but had escaped her in the bedroom with Josh. Her husband had left her sopping and while he went to the bathroom in their bedroom, she'd scurried out to the guest bathroom in the hall not sure why she wanted out of the bedroom so bad. But now it was apparent it was about finishing herself off in case Josh reneged on a round two after he came out of the bathroom, or wasn't able to get it up again.

The pad of her middle finger took over now, slipping inside herself while curling her clit against her palm at the same time. Her legs trembled as the orgasm finally told her it was on its way, and she pulled over a clean hand towel and bit it to stifle any sounds she wouldn't want Josh to hear.

The way she'd betrayed her husband today was a sin. It would never happen again because she just wasn't that kind of woman—but the events of the last few days were exhilarating in a way she couldn't even comprehend. And as the freight train of an orgasm rumbled down her tracks looking to pull into the station, she found herself thinking of another man. Thinking of his hands, how large they were, how masculine. Thought of how despite their size and strength they had remarkable well-groomed grace. She chomped the towel harder thinking of the way his black arm hair furred over the crisp razor edge of his expensive dress shirt, a shirt with French cuffs and gold links to hold them in place.

"Ah, mm, ah," she panted into the dampening cotton of the hand towel, seizing her eyes shut. But there in the darkness once again it wasn't her husband who loomed, it was another man. That man's hand touched her stomach, it went down under her pants and into her underwear and she let him, stood there dumbly wondering what his fingers would feel like inside her pussy.

"Mm, mm," she moaned into the towel as the orgasm came finally, roiling over the inside curve of her skull like a thundercloud pregnant with hot rain.

Her toes pushed right up, and she pressed her thighs together crushing her own hand against her pussy, her strangled cries swallowed up by the towel in her mouth. She snorted through her nose, catching her breath, two fingers pulsing against her button as the passion subsided. Now she could think of Josh, now she could picture him again, his pleasant face subsuming the face of the other man.

Blood thundered in her ears, and she could hear the hoarse whisper of her breath in her lungs. And now she was sure there was someone on the other side of the door.

Josh called her name, and she went still saying, "Just had to pee, Josh, I'll be right out."

"Okay."

Then she was sure he stood a long moment before returning to the bedroom. She whispered fuck and lightly thumped the heel of her fist against the cushioned curve of the toilet paper. If only she'd had the courage to tell Josh the truth. If only she'd not run from it. Maybe it wouldn't have been made worse today. She'd thought to spare her husband, but her silence only made everything worse. The other thing she could've done was tell Devlin there was nothing to talk about. Instead, she agreed to meet him.

7
AFTERNOON DELIGHT

Without planning to do it, she found herself in a hot shower midmorning, even putting her face and hair under the stream, thinking then, shit, she would have to dry her hair now. And she did that, too, looking vacantly at her reflection in the bathroom mirror, the whining of her hairdryer drowning out any errant thought about the lunacy of what she was doing.

Then it was 11 A.M., and she was in the family room with idle hands. She painted her nails in black, then with her heels on the couch on a spread out towel, she did her toes as well. The whole while she watched her soap opera on Netflix. But now it was lunch, and it was time she had to confront some things.

Was she really going to go out and meet Devlin?

Up to this point, though it was like she was on autopilot, everything she'd done this morning was noncommittal. She did need a shower. Hadn't washed her hair in a couple days, so that had to be done; sure, her nails were done last Saturday, not exactly chipping since then, but what if...? . . . Was it possible she didn't want Devlin to see her with the same nail polish three days later? Boy, that was like high school. Worried about those tiny little indicators and what they showed to those with watchful eyes. . . . *She's wearing that same outfit again, same color on her nails, her dad hasn't had a new car in five years* . . . "Shit," she said, putting her face in her hands, letting her black mane hang around her wrists, smelling like tropical coconut, the 2-in-1 shampoo from Costco she told Josh *not* to buy, and yet it was the exact one he bought. *I thought you said you* wanted *the 2-in-1.*

She couldn't go out to meet Devlin. Wouldn't. Though maybe she should, at least, *talk* to Devlin. But then again, maybe it was better to let it all go by. When Devlin had sent the message, her knee-jerk reaction was to ignore it—delete it and never respond. Let this nasty little grape wither on its vine and die, fall off and turn to fertilizer for someone else's story. But then she considered meeting with him and talking to him, maybe they could come to some sort of arrangement where they both would agree to ally, and if they stayed strong, they could say anybody claiming they saw anything or heard anything was just misrepresenting or misunderstanding. Then when—or maybe even *if*—Josh heard from someone, there would be some deniability. But then again, maybe meeting Devlin would make things worse.

Of course, it would make it worse. What was she thinking?

But then the apartment buzzer rang on the phone, that god damn awful buzzing sound left over from another decade that had her jolting right off the couch. She trotted quietly across the apartment like she was sneaking up on the squawk box, picking up the landline to see who was ringing her. It was Devlin, his distinct gravelly voice saying, "You coming down or am I coming up?"

She said, "What the hell are you doing here? You're in the lobby?"

"You don't have a car. Where were you going to meet me?"

How did he know whether she had a car or not? She said, "I don't want to talk to you, just go away."

"You said you wanted to talk to me."

"Not here."

"Come down to meet me."

"I'm not coming down, Devlin. Just go away."

After a dreadful, quiet beat, Devlin said: "You know we need to talk."

She stood there in the hall, biting her lip, knowing Devlin was right, they should talk, but also knowing she was right. *Just go away.*

"I can't come down," she said softly.

"Buzz me up."

Again, a knee-jerk reaction that made sense: No.

That's the worst idea possible. But then what? Go down and meet him? Some of the neighbors seeing her in the middle of the day with another man heading out for lunch? If it was mentioned to Josh, she would have to come clean. What if someone saw Devlin coming up to the apartment?

How would they know which apartment he was going to? And why do you think everybody's watching what you're doing?—talk about a guilty conscience.

She said nothing, pressed three, the button that would unlock the front vestibule door. Then she was hanging up, slamming the phone on the base, running to the bathroom and checking herself in the mirror.

This shaggy haircut she was sporting these days, what the hell was that? Bangs, but long ones that came right down over her eyebrows, practically touching her eyelashes sometimes. All puffy on top, shaggy too, her natural waves coming out as she got more mature, liking it at first, but now seeing her reflection in the mirror seeing some sort of strange 70s New York art scene poser, or, worse, was the hairstyle comedic?—maybe one of the guys from Spinal Tap. . . . She ran fingers into her mane, shook it loose, shaking her head and making a pouting face. Fucking lipstick, she thought, you need lipstick—but it was too late now to do that. She looked at her nails, glad she had done that at least. Then down at her toes, wiggling them on the bathroom tile. Black cotton pants, black tank top, it would have to do.

Then there was knocking on the door. Distinctly Devlin. Even the knock coming confident.

And she was doing that long-striding prance thing, going light on the balls of her feet, undoing the chain and turning the deadbolt. She opened the door a crack and saw Devlin standing in her hall, looking so wildly out of place.

THEY STARED AT EACH OTHER A LONG uncomfortable beat until Devlin finally said, "You going to invite me in?"

"Yeah," she said, still peeping through the gap in her door up at the man. She held the door in both hands, walked backward bowing graciously to him as if he were a welcome guest. Never even invited the guy to her house.

Devlin came in, hands in the pockets of his suit pants, eyes already moving around her apartment, picking out all its inadequacies, she was sure. She closed the door behind him, first poking her head into the hall, happy to see that Devlin hadn't been seen, then closed the door and locked it. She turned to Devlin, then turned right back and ran the chain across the door as well. *What was that—worry that Josh might show up for lunch, catch you two together?*

Now she was standing behind Devlin, him taking up a huge amount of space in their foyer. He was tall, maybe a full head above her, hair neatly trimmed at the back and the sides, brushed off his brow and temples in thick black waves. His suit was black, or maybe charcoal, a ghostly stripe in it that you had to look carefully for, the pant legs tailored, breaking nicely on monk-strap brogues that shone with polish. She came to stand beside him, folding her arms and tucking her hands in her armpits.

He was staring at the large framed photograph of the main entrance of the Lungshan Temple in Taiwan, a picture taken by her father from the temple's outer courtyard about twenty years ago. He said, "What's this?"

"A temple in Taiwan," she said, explaining the picture, "my dad took it." The photo was a moody black and white, high contrast, all bright sky, most of the temple's wall hidden in mysterious shadow, its bowed spine of a pagoda roof stark against the clouds.

Still examining the photo, Devlin said, "Family vacation?"

Now she felt stupid, the picture having a certain artistic quality she liked guests to see when they came in the front door, and now reduced to a dumb vacation photo her dad had taken. She said, "Not really a vacation. We stayed a couple months with family every summer."

"In Taiwan?"

She repeated, "I said the temple's in Taiwan."

He said no more, not wishing to engage in her bristly patter, smirking already as he stood straighter and faced her, showing a certain smug amusement.

"Yes, in Taiwan," she said.

He said, "Are we going to talk?"

"You're the one that wanted to talk, so talk," she said.

He chuckled, his eyes going over the family room now. He said, "How long you lived here?"

"I'm sorry," she said, "I didn't realize you're in the real estate game—this is a business call?"

"Just making small talk, Kimmy."

"I've got things to do today, Devlin. I know you do too. So why don't we just make this quick?"

He stepped deeper into the apartment, moving from the foyer into the mouth of the living room, and she followed, coming to stand beside him, leaning her back on the wall. He said, "I came here, Kimmy, because I wanted to apologize."

She chuckled, looking at his angular profile, its haughty attitude, but honestly surprised that he would say that. "Apologize to me? You know I'm surprised, right?"

"I should apologize, don't you think?"

She agreed. "Yeah, you should."

"Maybe I said some things over the line."

"Yeah, okay," she said. "Maybe I overreacted."

"We got pretty worked up," he said.

And just like that, she could hear the innuendo in his words and knew his apology was just greasy manipulation, him looking to see what more he could get from her. She crossed her arms and showed her loosest expression.

Devlin said, "You going to show me around?"

"Show you around my apartment? No."

He turned to face her finally, looking down at her and there was that aggravating smirk. A know-it-all superior expression on his face, studying her. He said, "Is Josh home?"

"Of course not. You think I'd agree to this if he was here?"

Devlin laughed again, light, but still with that gravelly arrogant sound. He eased off the wall, walked into the family room, looking into her kitchen through the pass-through. He said, "Where is Double-A today?"

"Who's Double-A?"

"Your husband."

"He's at work."

"Where's he work? Market research or something, right?"

"He's at A.J. Swanson."

"Mid-level management?"

"He's got twenty employees under him."

Devlin nodded, looking around the kitchen, putting his palms on the pass-through countertop, his big, well-manicured hands flat on the tile surface.

She said, "What's Double-A?"

Devlin turned, leaned an elbow on the counter-top, face turned away, looking out past the TV and beyond the windows to the bright sunny day, saying, "What we called Josh back in grade school."

"Why?"

"Locker room stuff—we used to say Josh's dick was like one of those little batteries you put in electronics."

She bristled, clucked her tongue, rolled her eyes and slumped against the countertop. "This shit again. You came here to apologize but pull the same garbage?" She scowled and shook her head at him. "Is it supposed to be attractive to people, telling them you've got a big dick?"

"I didn't say a thing about mine."

"That's the power of omission. Singling out someone disparagingly in an attempt to highlight the opposite factor in yourself."

Now he rolled his eyes. "It was grade school anyway, Kimmy. I'm sure Josh hit puberty just fine."

"My husband hit puberty just fine, Devlin."

Devlin smiled, and when their eyes met, there was an electric knowledge that zipped between them. While Josh may be fine, she was a lot more familiar with Devlin than what she let on. She looked away.

"Not quite what I heard."

She met his eyes. "You want to start a fight all over again? I'm not falling for it this time."

His smugness melted, and he made a happy, peaceful face. "Kimmy, I came here to be your friend. We let ourselves act badly on the weekend, me ten times more than you, and I'm here for you, for your sake."

"You'll pardon me if I don't quite believe you're here for benevolent reasons."

"What did you tell Josh?"

She looked at him like he was an idiot. "Nothing."

"Did you talk to anybody?"

She shook her head no.

"You talk to your friends?"

She shook her head no again.

"Are they gonna rat you out?"

She shrugged her shoulders, heavy depressive feelings settling on her. "I don't think so."

"Nothing happened. Isn't that right?"

"Nothing happened," she agreed.

"So we're good?"

"You tell me," she said, not looking at him.

"That's what I'm here telling you, Kimmy. Hey, come on, look at me."

She turned her face his way, her jaw set firm, the muscles in the corners near her ears bulging and flexing as the urge to strike him renewed. Only, he *was* behaving himself. *What could you be mad at him for now? Aren't you just mad at yourself?*

They stared at each other for a long time, and his eyes didn't move away. A slow smile began to creep on his face, and he said, "Look, I let things get out of hand because it felt *good* to let it get out of hand."

"It felt good to be an asshole?"

"You make me feel a certain way."

"Don't say that."

"It was exciting." He smiled.

"It's not going to happen," she said, looking in his eyes.

"That's fine," he said. "I had time to think, you know, put into perspective why maybe I said some of those things."

"And what's that perspective?"

"Of all the people from high school, Kimmy, do you know who matured the most?"

She knew he was going to say her, but she shrugged her shoulders.

He didn't even need to say her name, saying now, "You're one of those girls that was a kid in high school, but the way you are now…"

"What—I'm a grown woman?" she said sarcastically.

"Yes."

"Girls grow up, you know."

"Not those other girls, not the ones from high school. They never really changed much. They get set in their ways, get hitched or go nowhere, but not you."

She said, "If I show you around, will you go then?"

"Hey," he said, putting out his hand like he wanted to hold hers. "I'm serious, Kimmy. I'm not here to be a jerk. I'm trying to make things better. I know you're mad at me. Just work with me."

Before she knew it—just the way she'd found herself mindlessly standing under the stream of the shower—she put her hand in his. But he didn't creep her out, hold her delicately, caress her knuckles or anything like that. He shook her hand like they were making an agreement. Partners in crime, as it were.

"Yes," he said, looking in her eyes, "show me around, then I'll go."

Before heading down the hall with him, she paused, wringing her hands together nervously and saying, "Do you want a cup of coffee or something?"

Devlin said sure, and then watched her as she walked into the kitchen and filled the kettle with water. He stood behind her with his hands linked together on the pass-through counter, taking up a huge chunk of that space with his large frame. Devlin'd matured too. In high school, he'd been tall, and well-built from playing sports. Now that he was a man, he'd filled out. Not just handsome, not just physically fit, but a man with presence. The expensive suit, expensive haircut, the physical space he took up, the way he carried himself . . . There was unmistakable power in his presence, enough that he looked completely out of place in her simple apartment. She set the kettle to boil, saying, "I mean, I'll show you around. I don't know what you're expecting. It's not a big apartment."

"Humor me," he said, and she knew he was trying to get her into the bedroom. But she wouldn't go there.

She came around to the family room again, walking underneath him as he watched her, smirking, heading down the hall. She said, "This is Josh's office, no big deal," and kept going. But Devlin had stopped to look again, saying, "Josh is happy there? At Swanson."

"Yeah, he is."

"That's what he went to school for? Marketing?"

"Business," she said.

Devlin pushed himself off the frame, sauntered to join her. She pointed to the closed bedroom door, said, "That's our bedroom," saying it fast, then walking into the guest bedroom that had been converted into her Katt Basket room. The basket she'd started in the morning sat on her worktable like a reedy sunburst. The lights had been turned off, her space dim but navigable because of the bright summer day out the windows. She said, "This is where I make my baskets."

"Right," he said, arms folded, standing in her room next to her worktable, looking at the things on her shelves. He said, "You make these?" nodding his chin towards two baskets that were on the top shelf.

"I did."

He took one down, flipped it over, examined it. "That's amazing. You do this by hand, or is it a machine?"

"I weave them by hand."

"Are you serious?" he said, holding it up to the light now, the spiral pattern shadows cast from her basket playing on the angular ridges of his handsome face.

"My grandmother taught me."

"Is it Chinese or something?"

"Kind of," she said. "Taiwanese, Japanese influence."

"How much do you charge?"

"For a single basket?"

"Yeah," he said, placing it back on the top shelf where he got it from

"A hundred-fifty."

"How many can you make in a day?"

"One and a bit, sometimes two, but I'm happy just doing one."

He gestured at the bundles of reed grass, tied in manageable bunches with twine. "How much does this grass stuff cost?"

"Like what's my profit margin?"

"Yeah," he said, suddenly appearing to her like a financial manager.

She got defensive saying, "Look, Devlin, it's just a hobby."

"Didn't sound like a hobby when you were talking about it at Tiffany's. Sounded like you treated it as a business."

"Well, yeah, I treat it as a business."

"Can you get other people to make them for you?"

"It's kind of a hard skill to acquire."

"Are there machines that make them?"

She paused. "Yes."

"Would you sell your name?"

"No. That's not what I want to do."

"So all you'll ever make is $150 a day?"

"Look, when I wasn't pregnant anymore—"

"I'm not saying anything," he said. "I'm trying to be your friend."

"Making the baskets makes me happy, okay?"

"You're making them *for* someone. If making baskets makes you happy, you could sell the name, sit back on the profits, have fun making baskets for yourself. Best baskets anyone ever saw."

"I'm going to go back to work at some time."

"So that's the end of the basket company?"

"I don't know, Devlin. I don't really think about it."

"But you think about going back to work?"

"Of course."

Devlin took a deep breath, considering what she said and looking out their windows at the undulating boughs of tree tops and the street beyond. He said, "You come out of Western?"

"Yes."

"Law school?"

"Queens."

"Shit, Kimmy," he said.

"What?"

"You speak Chinese, don't you?"

"You know I do."

"I don't know that. I thought so, though."

"So what?"

"You know what I would pay a young lawyer who knew her shit, who didn't back down . . . *and* she could speak Chinese?"

"Right," she said, giving him a snide look. "The import export game."

"I have people that speak Chinese, but they're not half as smart as you are."

She looked away, vigorously scratched the back of her neck, making her hair flutter. She said, "I'm going back to my other firm."

"Immigration law."

"So?"

"Helping Chinese come over here, get them on their feet so they make more money than you?"

She made an exasperated sound, folded her arms and glowered at him.

He didn't wilt. "You know it's true."

"It's not true, Devlin. I help people. It's hard to navigate the rules, it's hard to find a reliable advocate who's looking out for you..."

"And who's looking out for you?"

"I am," she said. "Josh is."

"I'm glad," he said. "I think you're an incredible woman."

"Oh God," she said and rolled her eyes dramatically as a defense mechanism.

He said, "I do. You don't see it, but you're a killer in disguise. . . . The way you fought back...?"

She cocked her head and tried to look serious. "Did I scare you?"

"You know what it did to me," he said.

She didn't respond. Let it hang. Let it drop. Said nothing. "That's the grand tour, Devlin," she said. "You want that cup of coffee now?"

.   .   .

INSTEAD OF COMING INTO THE KITCHEN, DEVLIN stopped at the mouth of the family room, making her turn around. She crossed her arms, said, "What, you didn't get me into the bedroom so now you're going to leave? What about our coffee?"

"I came here to take you out, Kimmy. I wasn't trying to get into your apartment or your bedroom. I had something come up, I don't have a lot of time. Maybe next week you can come out for lunch with me and we'll talk business."

"Not likely," she said.

"That's up to you. I don't think you know what you've got."

"What have I got, Devlin?"

He strode toward her, and she hadn't expected it. She bumbled a step backward, her bare heel going off the hall carpet and onto the granite tile. Her back bumped against the wall. Devlin stood before her, looming over top of her, making her look up. He said, "You know."

"I know what?" Her skin tightened, her bravado waning.

"Deep down you know you're a lot more."

She whispered, "A lot more what?"

"You *want* more."

"I've got everything I want."

"That's why you're twenty-seven years old, making baskets?"

The argument it was her own company, her own rules, she was her own boss, was moot—he'd exposed the truth, flipped open her books with some simple mathematics. It was a fun business, but she had a law degree; she was hiding out in the apartment.

"I'm a good lawyer," she said.

"I bet you're good at everything."

"I am," she said.

When he brought his hand up to touch her neck, she grabbed his wrist, dug her nails into it. "Don't," she warned him.

"Next week when I come, I'll get you out of this place. What do you say?"

"I told you what I think."

He lifted his hand from where he touched her neck; she let his wrist go. But he ran two fingertips from her collarbone down over the cotton of her chest, his middle finger riding right over top of the hardened bud of her nipple, making her hiss a sharp intake of air . . . And his hand kept going, moving swiftly but softly, his palm resting on the flat of her stomach. Her mouth fell open, and she looked into his eyes. He ran his flattened hand low on her stomach, his fingers slipping under the waistband of her drawstring pants, right underneath her panties. She gasped, went on her tiptoes, pressed her back against the wall. And when he touched her at her core, she trembled and closed her eyes.

"I see the real you, Kimmy—am I the only one who sees that woman in there, that killer?"

"Don't," she said again, but made no move to stop him.

His two fingers pleasured her, stroking and pushing, making her wet, all happening so fast she couldn't believe it. He hooked those fingers. He had big fingers and the two of them went inside her together, as big as a dick. She let out a soft whimper, eyes closed, face turning away from him.

"Fuck, Kimmy, the woman you've become puts all those other girls to shame. You're all I thought about since Saturday."

His fingers plunged in and out of her; she had the strength, the resolve, now to bring her hands together and grasp his wrist. It took two hands to circle him, and she could feel the muscles flexing in his forearm as he pleasured her. Her calves and thighs trembled; instead of squirming away, she tried getting higher on her toes to make it harder for him to finger her. But he continued, making a low grumbling sound. When her eyes fluttered open, she found his eyes boring into hers.

"We can't," she said.

But her hands undid the knot on the front of her pants, and her thumbs pushed out the waistband to draw out the tightness of the string. The loosened pants fell around her ankles. The tightness of her panties, stuffed with Devlin's large hand, reminded her how bad what she'd just done was. She gripped the side strings of her panties, pulled them tight, trying to trap his hand inside them.

"No, don't," she said, but he still fingered her.

"You're so fucking wet," he said, "so fucking unbelievable," getting closer to her, not trying to kiss her —like he knew if his lips came near hers the spell would be broken, his fingers inside her somehow more acceptable than his lips on hers.

All she could do was whimper and complain, standing there getting fingered in her front hall when she swore there would be nothing that would happen between them, up on her toes, her hands going around Devlin now, slipping inside his jacket and feeling the muscle under the silky cotton of his expensive dress shirt. She hugged her cheek to his chest, everything from the waist down turning to liquid; if he stepped back, she would collapse on the floor.

"Fuck," she blurted, right hand snatching down between them, trying to find his big dick. It was down the side of his pant leg, half hard and so incredibly huge. She squeezed it, kneaded it, her grip in the middle.

Devlin's other hand came between them, his plunging fingers never stopping the pleasure he was delivering, finding his zipper and drawing it down. She slipped her hand inside the yawning opening of his boxers, desperate to hold his manhood. Her grip went around it, feeling the scratch of his pubic hair, the stickiness of his skin. He was so big.

He whispered, "I left you aching, didn't I? Kimmy didn't get what she needed."

"I don't need you."

He said, "Your pussy's wet like an overripe peach."

She swooned, her knees dipping; his fingers plunged deep with a loud squelching. Wet dripped her thighs. "Oh, fuck."

He said, "You want to come?"

"N-no."

He chuckled. "I can stop."

She closed her eyes and bit her lip. "Make me... Make me come."

There was a low animal sound in his chest, and she knew he studied her while he finger-fucked her. The feeling was incredible, her awful surrender to this man she didn't like shameful and overwhelming. Her back shimmied on the wall like she tried to escape him, but the truth was, it just thrust her pelvis against his hand. The heel of his thumb mashed against her clit and a sudden tightness seized between her legs. It felt like her stomach was a shopping bag with an anvil in it. "Oh God, oh no," she whined, and when she heard his chuckle, the lust grew tighter with anger. She clenched her teeth, said, "You lied to me."

He hummed a gravelly sound. "How?"

"You came here to get me in the bedroom."

His fingers slowed, and she moaned, her hips trying to move faster to make up for his retreat. Devlin said, "No, I didn't."

Her eyes fluttered open, and she met his steely gaze. She conjured defiance, sneered. "So you *don't* want to fuck me?"

"What I'm going to do to you will take us hours," he said, plunging into her again, fast and hard, the hump of his palm bullying her swollen clit.

"Oh God," she panted, gripped his arm, her other hand squeezing his huge cock.

"But instead I have to go to the airport."

"Good," she spat.

Another sly chuckle. "You don't want me to leave you like a rag doll in your bed?"

She gasped, moaned. "I'm married, Devlin."

"I just want to fuck you, Kimmy. We're not running off together."

She let his dick go, held his wrist with both hands, and went higher on her toes. "I'm *married*, Devlin."

Devlin still pleasured her, his strong hand working her insides to the release she hated she craved. "I want to give you what you need between your legs."

She whispered, "What's that?"

"I want to watch your face when you come. I want to see you wild . . . I want to see wild Kimmy."

"Yeah?" she let him go, her hands formed clumsy fists against her stomach; she stayed on her toes, squeezed her eyes shut and turned away from him. He had complete control of her with his fingers inside her, and now she completely surrendered; *make me come, Devlin, then get out.*

"Ah, ah, ah," she began to pant, "oh, oh no, mm, mm," her features scrunching, but what was oncoming would hopefully be a tidal swell that would wash away all the ache she had for him since Saturday. The deep sexual need for a man she hated and who wasn't her husband.

"You can come now, Kimmy. Show me how you come."

"Fuck off, oh, fuck you," she whined and complained, humping his hand and shaking her head from side to side, but at last it came. She shouted out, bit her lip to stifle such an awful sound from an awful woman, a sound so obvious and lusty. She grabbed his wrist again, her two hands holding him in place, the sharp edge of his cuff link digging into her palm.

"Look at that beautiful face, Kimmy, oh the pleasure," he groaned.

She moaned as the orgasm still warbled through her, aftershocks jolting her. Her legs went to jelly, and she almost collapsed. Devlin held her in place, and she fell forward against him to be supported so she wouldn't go to the floor. His arm circled her, the fingers of the other hand still inside her and now softly massaging the last tweaks of rapture from her.

"Fuck, Kimmy, mm," he said, "the things I'm going to do to you…" He bit her neck, and she dug nails into his back. Her right hand went below his belt, slipped into his fly, found his hard cock constrained in his suit pants and stroked. Now they were in her hall embraced like two high school kids at a school dance, hands in each other's pants, her jerking him. For what—*you want him to come?*

As the wild ravishment ebbed from her with each heartbeat, its absence was filled with regret and shame—she let him go and grimaced, pushed herself off till she had her back on the wall again. Her ass muscles quivered.

Devlin stood where he was; her eyes lowered and watched his big hands part his fly and pull out his huge cock. He let it go to watch her take it in, standing there in expensive brogues shoulder width apart, unreal manhood nodding side to side, a vein-scribbled column of hard man-flesh.

She whispered, "You want to fuck me?"

"I want you to have everything you need."

"You think that dick is all I need?"

Now he stepped toward her, cock bobbing. "I'm more than a big cock. . . . And I know you're curious what that means."

"I'm not," she said, her breaths coming faster.

"Don't lie, Kimmy. You wanted a lot more on Saturday."

She shook her head no, and he held her chin to look into her eyes. His cock was hot on her stomach, and she gripped it, began absently swiping it against her skin under her shirt. "Do you have a condom?"

He grumbled a small laugh. "You didn't ask for a condom at Tiffany's."

"I think I'm ovulating."

He breathed inward through his teeth; an appreciative sound, like her fertility aroused him. His hands went to her sides; he hoisted her up, and she yelped a small sound, her bare legs kicking, her pants falling off her feet, completely bottomless now as Devlin set her bare ass down on the hall table, the vase clunking, the dish of coins rattling. Her curved back pressed the wall, the framed picture her father had taken of the Lungshan Temple touching the crown of her head.

"We have to stop," she said.

Devlin ignored her, eyes glued to her bared pussy, getting between her legs, his cock on her thigh. He tugged up her shirt and exposed her stomach. She sunk it in even though she was a skinny girl, and when he lifted her shirt higher, she stopped him, afraid he would expose her breasts. Her nonexistent breasts that all Devlin's high school hookups liked to poke fun at in the locker room—oh so good-natured of course: *Why, Chinese girls just don't have big breasts*, their unkind words implied.

Now she saw how wet he'd made her; could see the shine inside her thighs, see droplets beaded in her patch, and wanted to close her legs—but he was between them.

"We can't," she whispered. "You have to go."

Devlin put his cock on her stomach and she groaned at the sight of it against her skin, the size of it, marveling how it could fit in her tight space, and how deep it would go. He ran the base into the slick cleft of her sex, over her opening and putting pressure on her clit; her head went back and clunked the Temple, knocking it askew. "Oh God," she sighed.

"Fuck, Kimmy, I want in this pussy so bad."

"I can use my hand," she negotiated.

"Look how bad you want it," he said.

"I don't," she said and gripped his cock. She choked it, watched the huge flared shape of his glans deepen in color, a sick knot tightening above her stomach. He ran it through her grip, and she turned her chin up to see what Devlin Stone's face looked like when he was pleasured. His steely eyes glowered on hers, his jaw set hard, breathing steady through his nose as his size spread her slippery grip. She began to jerk him a little faster, wanting to see his eyes roll, or his mouth hang open. But instead he thumbed his cock down so when he stroked it through her grip the underside ran over her hot furrow like a boat's hull dragged up a beach.

"Mm," she whimpered as white bulbs of light flickered in the sides of her vision.

Devlin pulled his hips right back like he would try to put it inside her, and she pleaded with her eyes not to do that to her. Her fingertips aimed the cock head into her opening and now she dared him to take control, make him the one responsible for her badness.

With his hips, he thrummed easy pulses of his cock against her, spearing her opening but not entering into her body. It got her knees rising, wanting him to be inside her again. She caressed the top of his cock and held his gaze.

"I need a condom," she said, not sure if it was

meant to end the effort or a genuine request that if one were available they could proceed.

"I have to go to the airport," he said.

She grunted at the punch that gave her, the double whammy: They weren't going to fuck (shouldn't that be a *Thank God?*), and the embarrassment Devlin had more self control than her. "Go," she said, firm.

That made him smile, and she had the urge to lash out at his smug face again, hating that he'd got her to submit, looking to blame him for her own weakness. "Fucking go," she said and backhanded his cock away from her pussy.

Devlin leaned over her, looking like he would kiss her, and again she turned her face. Her hands gripped his upper arms, nails digging in; his arms were thick and so hard under the fine wool of his suit. He said, "I'm coming next week."

"No."

"Yes." He ran his cock up her pussy, the tip of him stroking into her navel.

"I want you to leave."

"You want me to fuck you. Stop acting like you *don't* want it." That made him chuckle, and he lifted off her. He stood before her, smiling wide. He unbuckled his belt, unzipped his pants, struggled to hide his erection under the fabric, then zipped them closed again.

She said, "You're going?"

Devlin did up the belt buckle. She closed her

thighs, feeling more naked now he was clothed. A married woman sitting on her hall table, her pants who-knows-where, her pussy smeared with only her own sexual product. She slipped herself off the table to stand, then tugged down her shirt to cover her nudity, but the shirt wasn't long enough.

"I'm not the enemy," he said.

"Go to the airport," she said, crossing her arms, her thighs closed together, wet and warm, toes curling on the hall carpet.

"You and I are on the same side."

"No, we're not, Devlin."

He stepped closer, loomed over her. She looked up. He said, "Next Tuesday I'm coming back. I'm getting the bedroom door open and we're going to take care of that deep ache you have." His hand touched between her legs and she jumped.

"I don't have an ache," she said, her voice sounding thin and useless. But she began to squirm at his touch, feeling his fingertips stroking at her entry. "And I need you to go."

"Fuck, Kimmy," he sighed, "If I weren't flying to Vancouver, the things I would to you on that bed." He stepped away, showed her the shine on his fingers. He tugged his pocket square out, wiped his hand as he turned to the apartment door. "See you next Tuesday, Kimmy."

"I won't be home, Devlin," she said.

He smiled like he liked the answer—liked it

because he didn't believe it. He opened the door and left quietly.

She waited a beat, sighed, groaned, "Fuck," slouched, and had a huge and sudden urge to sleep. But, with her arms still folded, she crossed the apartment without her pants on, padded to the windows that looked down over the parking area, kneeled one knee on the seat of a chair and watched. In a moment she saw him two stories below, moving silently across the asphalt, the wind rustling his thick head of hair, loosing one curled strand that bounced as he walked. Devlin combed it back with his hand, blipped the alarm on his black Mercedes roadster parked on an angle taking up two visitors parking spaces.

She whispered, "Fucking asshole."

As the car lit up, and Devlin rolled out of their apartment complex, she moved back from the window so she wouldn't be spotted. When he was gone, she went to her pants, put them on, flopped on the couch. Tears threatened to come, but they never did. She lay in the silence, pushing back at her thoughts, afraid to face them, and in fifteen minutes her hand was slipping under her pants again, into her panties. She masturbated, writhing on the couch, imagining things had gone another way, her long legs moving up and down, heels sliding on the leather. After she came, the ache remained. Fucking Devlin.

She scrubbed the mess she'd left on the hall table, polished it. Tidied, checked for evidence of Devlin's presence. She lay back down on the couch, face furrowed and mean, hating herself. She fell asleep chewing the inside of her cheek.

* * *

AND NOW HERE SHE WAS AGAIN, USING HER HAND to find something, trying to chase away an aching need. Washing her hands in the bathroom sink, she looked at her eyes in the mirror. What was Devlin doing to her? The ache was real. A deep and insistent sexual longing she couldn't shake. Never had it before in her life. Not since high school, at least, that night with Amy and Devlin. Now it was back, and she didn't know what to do. She had a loving husband who she loved in return. She had a great sex life, didn't she? Josh satisfied her, and maybe once a week she'd do the deed herself at home alone making baskets and the urge hit her. But since Saturday there was an unshakeable hunger between her legs. The last man on earth she ever thought would be in her life again was now stuck like a sliver.

She dried her hands on the towel, flicked off the light, went into the hall.

Josh was waiting for her.

"Shit," you scared me she said and Josh smiled.

He leaned on the hallway wall, shirtless and wearing pajama pants. He wanted to show her something, his eyes indicating downward. His erection poked out his pajama pants, and he gripped it now, squeezing. She smiled, but grimaced. In that moment her first thought was Double-A and how the boys had teased her husband about his small penis just like the girls had teased her; the two of them sharing a unity in their sexual under-development.

But Josh was grown now, and his size had never entered her mind until she was re-introduced to Devlin Stone. Her hands had been all over another man today, and part of his allure was the pure masculine power that dangled between his legs.

Josh said, "I'm going to do terrible things to you, Kimmy," giving her a mean scowl but smirking.

"Told you I napped today," she said.

Josh pulled down the front of his PJs to show her his hardness. He was proud of it. Since the weekend he'd sputtered sexually and that wasn't like him. She was glad to see him renewed. She stepped into his space, put her hand on what he presented, feeling him hard as stone. The size difference was pronounced; this afternoon she'd tried to jerk off another man who was incredibly hung. She groaned at the psychic pain, and fell against the man she loved deeply, kissing his neck and jerking his cock.

Josh whispered, "You ready for me?" He kissed her cheek, ran his hands on her ribs.

"Come on and show me what you can do," she whispered, took his hand and led him back into their bedroom.

This is episode 1 of 15 in a long series describing dangerous sexual madness and awful betrayal.

This is only the beginning!

Sign up for my newsletter on my website to get the latest info, sneak peeks at upcoming stories, and even a free story or two down the road!

Visit my website!
ktmorrison.com